KEEP A COOL HEAD
&
A WARM BOSOM

a novel

By

DAVID KARLI

Brunswick

First Original Edition

Published in the United States of America

by

BRUNSWICK PUBLISHING COMPANY
LAWRENCEVILLE, VIRGINIA 23868

KEEP A COOL HEAD
&
A WARM BOSOM

Adolph Teitleman worked as a janitor at the liquor store at Ninth and Girard Avenue in one of the first-changed sections of North Philly. He was white and at one time did clerical work. He was nearing sixty and was slightly bent.

Adolph was sweeping the aisle close to where Joe Clark was stocking the bins with wine, and he took a letter out of his jacket pocket and showed it to Joe. It was signed "Your loving niece, Jeanne."

Joe read the letter then handed it back to Adolph saying, "This is hot stuff." He then gave a quick, austere glance at Adolph. "Your niece, eh?"

"Yeah. Her husband was killed in Korea. He was a general, and my niece is very depressed.

"It's a sad situation," Joe lamented.

"She begs for some loving everytime she sees me. Here's her picture, Joe."

Joe took the picture and studied it for a moment. "She's really nice," he commented.

"I try to help her out, but I'm no good with any woman, Joe." Adolph's words choked a little.

"Didn't you tell me you were married?" queried Joe.

"I was married for thirty years. My wife died ten years ago, so I thought I'd give it a whirl, but I can't get started." Adolph pushed the broom a little harder.

"Have you tried vitamins?" Joe was trying to be helpful.

"Plenty," Adolph answered quickly. "I tried a lot of things, including a lot of stuff we sell in here, but nothing seems to work. Do you know Herby who used to work in here?"

"Yeah," Joe nodded.

"Well, he got me a box of those Red Rooster pills." Adolph gave a sly look then continued, "I took a whole box of them, and all they did was make me go to the toilet." He shook his head and shrugged his shoulders.

"How about the doctor? Have you seen him yet?" asked Joe, trying to be helpful.

"Oh yeah, he gave me a special diet and told me to take vitamins, but it was still no soap." Adolph started to use the dust pan.

Joe lifted his hands as he though of something, "Just a minute, Adolph. Have you talked to that guy who comes in here carrying a burlap bag over his shoulder? He goes fishing every day."

"Freddy the Fisherman?"

"Right. He told me if he misses one day of lovin' he can't see straight."

"He said the same thing to me. He's the guy who told me to try Red Rooster pills and vitamin E, but I must be immune for it was another failure." Adolph looked forlorn.

"Would you want me to ask George or Jim if they know of anything?" George and Jim were clerks who worked in the same liquor store.

"Please no, Joe, I don't want too many people to know my problem, but thanks for the help." Adolph was finished in the aisle and moved toward the front of the store.

"Look who's coming in," Adolph nudged Joe, who was finished stocking the bins and moving toward the register.

Freddy stepped to the counter and asked, "A bottle of good sauterne wine. It will be good with the catfish I just caught. Did you ever eat them?"

"Oh yeah, I'm from up state. We had plenty of catfish and they are good eating," Joe agreed.

"I like to keep my hands busy, and that's why I go fishing," Freddy continued. "Do you have any kids, Joe?"

"My boy is twenty now — hardly a kid," Joe answered.

"Well, I have a boy who is twelve and a girl, fourteen," bragged Freddy.

Adolph took one hand from his broom and slid it into his pocket, saying, "Suppose they want to play with themselves?"

"Why, you dirty old man. I thought you would come up with some words of wisdom," Freddy ribbed, "but actually you're proving the point. The statistics say that rape victims range from eighteen months to eighty years. If the kids didn't play, who can say there would be less rape jobs?"

Freddy took his sauterne and headed for home.

George Dallas was a man in his fifties, and had been a cop for eight years. He left the police force fifteen years earlier, trying various jobs — post office, supermarket and a large drug store before coming to the liquor store. That was two years ago. He was disenchanted with the police, and he sometimes talked about things that happened while he was a cop.

Jim Smith, who worked along with George at the checkout stand, was of medium height, wore a mustache and his hairstyle was semi-afro. He had seven years in the liquor business, most of them in this store.

Jim had a great deal of respect for a policeman, and was planning on taking the exam for patrolman. He knew there was a good chance for advancement because a black member of the Police Department had just been promoted to Deputy Commissioner.

Both George and Jim were working the early shift on a Tuesday in July, but business was not really jumping.

"Jim," George said with a note of concern. "They'll bust you like they did me."

"Hey, wait a bit. I didn't take the exam yet and already you're my advisor," snapped Jim. "Seriously though George, you know I'm getting tired of waiting on these winos. Friday and Saturday nights kill me, and the main thing is that a cop at the start gets the same salary as a top manager in these stores."

A lady of about thirty-five walked in and George went over to wait on her. She had bronze skin, a nordic nose that suggested some modeling agent would be glad to pick her up and wore a striped halter and a white brief. She spoke quietly as she ordered her liquor and slipped a little note to George before leaving.

"Does that pretty gal want somebody to shack up with her?" Jim asked, smiling.

George read the note, then looked at Jim. "Jim, you must be a mind reader."

"Don't forget you're a married man," Jim warned.

"A little extra fun won't hurt," George laughed. It was slow so George kept on talking. "Did I ever tell you about the queer partner I had when I was on the police force?"

"Start telling me — I'll stop you if I heard it before," Jim smiled.

"Well, he was really friendly and he told me he liked the way I was built. That was about sixteen years ago, mind you. Anyhow, he had a hobby of taking odd photos. This guy wanted to take pictures of me while I was on the John! I asked him if it was for a new kind of center-fold.

"He answered 'No centerfold, just a form of art I'm interested in.' I asked him why he didn't approach some of the winos. They would be glad to do it if they got paid, but he said he didn't care to photograph them because they were in bad shape. I told him I wasn't interested in his idea of art. I asked for and got a new partner."

The liquor store was in a predominately black neighborhood, with only one white clerk working there.

Jim recalled the black clerk named Henry who used to work in the store. Henry got a bang out of talking to the white waitress who worked in the corner restaurant. His talk was saccharin, but the blonde didn't mind because Henry left a bit tip. One day Henry was waiting on a white man when the white waitress walked by. He pointed to the girl, saying, "That's my girl."

"What's so unusual about you having a girl friend?" the man stated, then added, "Now if that was a dude walking by it would be unusual."

Henry was nonplused, and from then on he didn't talk about having a white girl friend.

Jim also remembered Herby, who worked in the store a few years back. Herb was the suave type, very handsome and neatly dressed.

"If you see a damp cloth in the men's room, don't disturb it," Herb warned Jim. His explanation was, "I use the cloth to ease the trouble I have with a case of piles."

Jim didn't think too much about the cloth until a day they were taking inventory. A clerk found a pint of gin in a box of old shoes in the men's room and showed it to the manager. The manager checked the gin and discovered it had been watered down. He hastened to the bin where the gin was stocked and found three more pints that had been weakened with water.

Jim then knew why Herb wanted the damp cloth. He used it to soak off the capsule that protected the cap on the bottle. Herb would take off the capsule and turn the cap off, then he would take a drink and fill the bottle with water.

Herb was evidently unable to get the bottle back on the shelf in time, so he dropped it into a shoe box.

The manager questioned the clerks, but Herb would not admit he was guilty even after Jim challenged him by saying, "You are the only one I know who likes gin that much."

Herb did not confess until he was tricked. Late one night when only the manager and Herb were in the store — the manager purposely allowed the other clerks to go home — the manager called in an auditor. The auditor and the manager checked the money, and although the money was okay, they said it was short $200.

Herb denied taking the money, which was the truth, but when the auditor asked questions about the gin, Herb confessed.

The manager didn't want to lose Herb, so asked him to only pay for the spoiled gin, but Herb would not pay. He was more interested in getting a job with the cabs.

It was lunch time for Jim, and he went to the corner restaurant where he met Herby inside.

"How do you like your new job?" Jim asked.

"Great, Jim. I'm doing good on tips, and I don't have to worry about getting a hernia. I make a little less money from the whorehouses than I did when I started handling the jobs. I didn't work long before I got a list of joy houses. I get three dollars on every ten the guy spends.

"But the madams started worrying about accepting cab jobs. They said the cabs in front of the house were dead giveaways."

The waitress brought Jim's coffee, and after he took a gulp, Herb continued. "We were then told to park our cabs a block away and walk the client back to the house. That worked for a while until the supervisors noticed too many unattended cabs, so now if a driver is caught, his profits are cut." Herby buttered a roll.

"I'm lucky, Jim," he went on." I'm in right with two madams, Minnie the Fish and Rosie the Hips, so I do all right. A practical joker got me one time though. He gave me an address on Green Street and told me to ask for Kitty. One night I took a job there and found out that the place was a cat refuge."

Herby got up to leave, their lunch period being over. "See you later," he called to Jim as he left.

Back at the counter at the store, Jim told George of meeting Herby, but George interrupted. "Did you get your application for the test yet?"

"Yeah, George, but you never told me why you got busted."

"Well, the higher-ups claimed that my partner and I were involved in a robbery for our own profit, and they gave us a choice of resigning or they would press charges. We resigned because we didn't feel like fighting City Hall."

"You resigned?" Jim asked with a trace of cynicism.

"Don't believe me then," George said, moving to wait on the lady just entering. She wore a low cut house dress.

"A bottle of rock and rum," she ordered.

George got the bottle and placed it on the counter. "Anything else?"

"That will be all." The lady was middle aged and attractive.

George rang up the sale and bagged the bottle. He looked at her quizzically, then said, "Don't I see you at the 21 Bar?"

"I stop in with Sam once in a while," she admitted.

"Sam's your husband?"

"Right."

"This stuff is supposed to turn you on," George said as he pointed to the bag.

"It's for Sam," she answered, dryly. "He'll try anything, but I think there is a dead bird in the nest."

George laughed softly, as others began to gather around the cash register.

After the line thinned out, Jim said, "I thought she was going to slip you a note."

"I know what Sam looks like," George answered. "There may be a dead bird in the nest, but there is a hefty wallop in the fist."

"Look at these two coming in. I'm not sure that they are dudes."

The two walked playfully toward the counter. The first one wore lots of perfume, and he smiled broadly at Jim. His long slender fingers moved along the counter as though he were playing the piano.

"How about a bottle of Homo Seltzer," he wisecracked. "You know what that is? Ha ha. Remember the commercial 'Relief is just a swallow away!' "

"Ha," Jim nodded. "May I help you?"

"I'll take a pint of blackberry brandy. I want to warm up." He nudged his friend, and the pair walked out arm in arm with the brandy.

"The queen was right," George commented. "We sell much more of that brandy in the winter."

What gets me is I always thought ginger was a warmer-upper, however, we sell more ginger brandy in the summer."

"True, I noticed that," said George as he glanced at his next customer.

"Give me a bottle of blood," the guy ordered. He wanted either a port or a red sweet grape wine. His face was flushed, and what appeared to be a stocking was wrapped around his head. His dress was untidy, and he had a two-day beard.

The red wine would make him feel good. He thought it gave him blood for the blood he had just sold, but the wine was a poor substitute for a transfusion. It would increase the blood pressure — any red wine would do that.

"He looks like he's not wrapped too tight," commented George as the man walked out.

"He's had a rough life," Jim agreed.

"He sells his blood then buys the wine so he can sell more blood. Boy, what a life."

"One thing about him," Jim added, "he's not robbing." I'm thinking of a would-be John Dillinger who tried to rob the store on Fifth Street where I worked for a short while. The manager had placed a big pail of red paint under a window in the back of the store. It was the favorite place for the robbers to break in.

"A cop caught him trying to take a case of liquor out through the window, and although his pants were full of paint, he said he was not trying to rob the place. He said he needed some liquor and the store was closed! I don't think that guy will ever try to break in that store again."

Jim greeted a girl with an oval face as she stepped to the counter. "May I help you?"

"A bottle of tequila," the girl ordered. She had long black hair and wore leotards. Her costume increased the image of great strength in her thighs.

As the girl left, Jim turned to George and asked, "Did you see that?"

"How could I miss? She is a Puerto Rican and her name is Rosita."

"How do you know her name?" Jim queried.

"A bartender at the 21 Bar told me. He also said one of the patrons told him it's a wonder she was never raped. The bartender replied, 'If anybody tried to rape that girl, she could kick him to death.' "

A college dude, wearing a pin-striped tie, tight pants and two-tone shoes sauntered in. "Do you know what extrapolate means?" he asked.

"Yeah," offered Jim. "It means if you know a certain fact or set of facts you can use it in determining the solution of a similar problem."

"Right man. What are you doing in here? You should have a bigger job. Now, if you want to extrapolate on the women's lib thing, I'll ask the question. Do you think it won't be long before men will be the rape victims?"

"I can't see why it hasn't already happened. Some of those dudes with the long hair look pretty good," George said.

"You got something there!" exclaimed the dude before walking out.

"I'll stick with the females," insisted Jim, smiling.

George took a bundle of money back into the office for the manager to check and deposit it in the safe. When he came back to the counter, Jim said to him, "Look at this fellow. First he appears bent and sad, and as he gets closer to the store, he is straightening up and his face is getting brighter, and that's before he takes a drink."

"Yeah, I guess half the fun is buying the stuff," George agreed.

Everybody was not happy, however. Some of the elderly were being knocked down and their bottles taken from them. The victims of the muggings were mostly poor people who should not be deprived of their daily nip.

CHAPTER 2

Thursday was a great day for the winos, for evidently the next day was payday. One of the first customers had trouble breathing, and the guy in back of him tried to cheer him up.

"Nobody breathes easy all the time," he said. "That's the way life is, and when you do breathe well, it's a grand feeling. I heard vitamin B12 will help. Why don't you ask the doctor if it's okay to take it?"

"Thanks, I'll do that. I'll try anything to get relief," the man said as he wheezed.

A big superman, dressed in showy clothes was the next to come in. He gave the feeling that he had something on top of the wine as he said, "I'm gonna be a big man — the greatest. You just wait and see. Some day you'll hear about me — yeah. I'll be way up on top, and when I go to another country, what do you think they're gonna do? I got it all figured out, man. They're gonna do the same thing they did for Elizabeth, you know, the queen. When I arrive they'll perfume the streets I travel on. That's what they did for the Queen when she visited Canada."

George laughed and put the wine in the bag for Superfly, as he knew the streets were anything but perfumed. In fact, a gang of hoodlums had gone by in the early morning and had thrown a few buckets of garbage through a store window. Guards on the window had helped in reducing the damage, but there was still some garbage in the street — so was the aroma.

George then waited on a white man. He was about forty-five, thinning hair and had sideburns.

"I'm writing a book," the man spoke up, "and trying to define intelligence in a part of the story. I boil it down to simply doing something you have done before, like moving your pawn to king four to start a game of chess. Do you play chess?"

"No, I'm a checkers man, myself. I like to jump," George smiled.

"That's a good game too, but I'm hooked on chess now."

"Albert, my son, plays chess, but I don't know whether he's in your class," said George, brightly.

"Maybe he could stop in my store and we could try a few games. My place is just one block down at 825 Poplar."

"I'll tell him when I get home, and thanks."

"My name is Al too, but it stands for Alfred," he said and left the store.

Slick Willie came in ten minutes later. He was so slick he could take off his socks without removing his shoes. He had a dimpled chin and fuzzy sideburns, and wore a turtle neck sweater and high heel shoes.

"A bottle of Creme de Cacoa," he ordered, adding, "Do you know what I do with this?"

"What do you do with it," asked Jim, although he was sure he heard the answer before.

"I pour it over ice cream. It's out of this world," drooled Willie. "You oughta try it."

"I'll try it," promised Jim.

"You won't regret it," Willie assured before making his exit.

Willie was not really a pimp, but he had a gimmick. What he does is fix up girls, usually on welfare, with a meal ticket, then he gets in touch with a guy who owns a food store, or just works in a store and is willing to pay for the girl's meal. He introduces the guy, and it's all set. The guy and girl like the idea, and they are happy. Willie gets his cut from the girl — that's why he's called Slick Willie.

It had been a long grinding day. It was nearly six o'clock when Jim murmured to George, "Here comes your friend, Herby. I guess he ran out of gin."

"Hello, everybody, anybody going to lunch?"

"I'am going," George spoke up, walking toward the back of the store to wash up.

George and Herby walked through the revolving door of William's lunch room and sat at the nearest table.

A blonde, almond-eyed girl took their order. She had kewpie doll features and wore a turquois mini skirt.

"I'll have vegetable soup and a roll," George spoke up.

"Coffee?" she asked.

"Oh, yeah."

"Make mine a chicken salad sandwich and coffee," said Herby. Then turning to George, he said, "When you went back to wash, I was telling Jim about the wino who thought I was trying to take his place in line. The wino said he didn't want to borrow any of my stink, so I told Jim I said to the wino, 'Shut up you bastard.' Jim thought I used rough language, but I told him that kind is heard on TV."

"That's right Herby, but I can remember thirty years ago when I went to the burlesque show and the girls were not allowed to use the word 'leg' on the stage. If 'leg' appeared in the song the girl would bleep it out, and the orchestra would fill in with a drum roll," George recalled.

Herby took a bite of his andwich, then said, "That was before my time, but if you want to hear some language, you ought to get on the cabs. The drunks can really get on your nerves. You know what I do now? Well, I was rolling down 29th Street when I heard some drunks screaming for a cab, so I looked back. One was signaling me to back up, but instead I tried a little psychology and went forward just a little. If they had acted all right, I would have backed up for them, but they started to curse, one of them being 'Come back here, you yellow bastard,' so I disappeared quickly. I wouldn't handle them even if they paid me double." Herby drank some coffee then continued, "I'm thinking of taking the cop's exam. The pay is really good."

George let the spoon drop down from his mouth, spilling his soup. "Jim is waiting to take the test,"

"Tell him I wish him luck," Herby added, taking another bite.

"You really go for gin, don't you?" George didn't wait for the obvious answer. He grinned and said, "I prefer vodka, it's distilled twice, you know,"

"Yeah, I know, Bloody Marys, eh?" asked Herb.

"Not really. I like the screw drivers better." George laughed lightly and had another spoon of soup. "Talking about Bloody Mary's, did you notice the brand of vodka that substitutes the term, 'Red Dot' for Bloody Mary in their recipes?"

"Can't say I did," Herby responded quickly.

"Well, one day the boss of the place where they bottle that vodka came to the store and told me why he used Red Dot. He said his wife was named Mary and that was the reason he would never refer to the combination of tomato juice and vodka as a Bloody Mary."

"It's a wonder the other bottlers didn't follow suit. There must be some Marys in their families," remarked Herby.

"It must not bother them much," answered George, finishing his lunch.

They both got up from their chairs and paid their checks and returned to the store.

After Herby got his gin, George waited on the next customer. How are you, Doc?" He got a kick out of the doctor's favorite saying that the bottle he was buying was the reason he stayed alive.

The doctor's hair was turning a distinguished white. His brow was furrowed, and his chin was firm. He wore a neat tweed suit. As he leaned over the counter as though to obtain some privacy, he said, "My neighbor asked me if I thought some whisky would be good for him. The gentleman has hardening of the arteries, so I told him it never has been proven that whisky was beneficial, but he could try a little if he cared. It might help him forget he is sick." He then said in parting, "It's not the arteries that I need to be hard."

George looked up and recognized the girl that ordered creme de cacoa which she would probably pour on ice cream.

The only reason the president wants his two hundred thou is he wants to make sure he makes more than a hooker," she said while George bagged the bottle.

George smiled and handed it to the lady. She had lots of eye make-up on and was built high front and back.

After she left, George winked at Jim, and said, "Herby said she works for Minnie the Fish. He said she likes to take it in the head to make money." George winked again.

"Real business like," rejoined Jim.

"Oh, yeah, but to change the subject, do you know there is a johndarm staked out in here at night?"

"Johndarm?" Jim looked puzzled.

"Yeah, a cop is in here. The cops are really mad. You know we've been robbed three times this month, and the last time they cut in from the roof. They took nothing but the most expensive whisky and two cases of half pints. They gave the half pints to the neighbors to keep them quiet."

"Maybe I can watch him and gain some experience," Jim laughed for he knew he wouldn't be allowed to watch.

"Look who's coming in. I tell you, this business gets worse as the night grows older," George warned.

The worse was Jake the Fake. He was in bad need of a shave, and his face was scarred and weather-beaten. His clothes were in dire need of a seamstress.

"Friends, Rummies and countrymen," he greeted. "What's happening?" Then in a lower tone he said to George, "I picked up a dozen today."

After Jake went out with his bottle of tokay, George explained the cryptic remark to Jim. "He said he picked up a dozen. You know what his thing is? He goes out to the Schuylkill River and fishes out any condoms floating around. He takes them home and washes them out, dries them, puts a little powder on them and then he's all set to sell them. That's how he gets money for his wine."

"I guess I've heard everything now!" exclaimed Jim.

"Yeah, he ought to put one on his head. It really needs protection," George declared.

The next customer was Max Miller, one of the old timers. He had trouble walking with a cane. He came in to buy a half pint of whisky, which he would nurse along for three weeks — a teaspoon in the morning and a teaspoon at night. He missed the little restaurant that used to be near the market and the synagogue.

As Mr. Miller walked slowly away from the store, George remarked, "You know, Jim. The first time I waited on Max, he told me about the breakfast he used to get right after his morning prayer in the synagogue. He would have a big slice of salty herring, a large slice of onion, a boiled potato, rye bread and glass of tea, then he would go home and down the teaspoon of whisky."

At one time the neighborhood was Jewish. Two blocks east of the store was what was left of a colorful market, with push carts lining the sidewalks. Every week a store or two would move and a push cart or two would disappear, for they couldn't take it anymore. The big money families left because they had been scared.

"Not for me," said Jim in reference to Miller's breakfast. "It would make me too thirsty."

"Yeah, Max had long hair and a beard before the hippies were born." George smiled.

There was a broadcast the next day about what happened with the cop who was the stake-out. It had leaked out that a cop was stationed in the store overnight, and a hippie got an idea that worked. He knew that the cop was a ladies' man, so he took his girl — she was really wrapped tight — to the store at eleven P.M. She tapped on the window, and when the cop saw the beauty, he fell like two thousand pounds hardware. After an interval, there was another tap on the window, and this time it was the girl's boy friend. The cop let them haul two cases of the best liquor away in his car.

Since the store was on a constant inventory check, the cop lost his job.

"Don't play around with women while you're on duty," George suggested. "You see what happened to that man."

"He was nutty enough to take a chance, so now he suffers," Jim said, "but I don't have to worry about nooky. I have a wonderful wife."

A small commotion grasped the attention of George and Jim. Charlie the wino was bad-mouthing a guy because he wouldn't give him a dime toward buying a bottle.

"I heard all about you, you prince P-R-I-C-K," Charlie spelled it out. He then added, "You louse."

The guy he was giving it to couldn't take any more, so he ran out of the store, then Charlie performed an impromptu dance to the counter. "Did you see the punk who just ran out? Well, I know some of they guys he goes fishing with — they all go out in a small boat. His friends told me he's so cheap that when it's time for lunch, he takes sandwiches out of a bag, takes his penis out of his pants then rubs it all over the sandwiches. He wants to make sure the guys won't ask for something to eat. Can you beat that?" Charlie pointed to Jim.

"I've got to agree with you, Charlie," Jim laughed.

"How about a dime, then I can make a bottle. That's all I need," insisted the wino.

Jim slipped a dime to Charlie, althought it was against the rules. Charlie danced out with his bottle of juice.

"Did you hear from the civil service yet?" asked George after the customers were all gone.

"No," answered Jim, "but I been over to the bookstore and got a book on sample questions they ask in the test." He handed the book to George.

"I didn't have those kind of questions." George handed the book back. "They're getting tough. Maybe they want college men on the force."

"That's what I heard," Jim rejoined.

"Wow! Look at this guy staggering in," George exclaimed. "He won't get anything, 'cause he's already loaded."

The souse tried to attract Jim's attention.

"I'm sorry sir. Come back later. I can't serve you now," Jim said, sympathetically.

"What do you mean, later?" slurred the drunk.

"Just later. I'll see you later." Jim was trying hard to be nice to the tippler.

"You think I'm drunk, don't cha?" said the liquid voice. "Well, you're like the guy who didn't know a hole in the ground from something else, if you know what I mean. You see, the guy tried to get a job as a gravedigger. He used to work in a hospital as an orderly. Sometimes he gave a patient an enema, so he didn't know whether he was digging or taking care of the patient's needs. How do you like those apples?"

The office manger heard the commotion and came out and quietly escorted the guy to the door.

"What a character," the manager said. He was a short stocky man, immaculately dressed.

"He likes to tell dirty jokes," added Jim as he pinched his nose.

It was time for Jim to take his lunch break, and he met Herby at Williams. After ordering a hamburger and coffee, Jim opened the math book to the page where the tough questions were.

"Oh yeah," said Herby. "It's strange that they are straight questions and not multiple choice, the kind that were so popular. For instance, this question — ten to the zero power = ? The answer is One. If it was given as a multiple choice question, you would pick from the following:

1) -10 2(10) 3(.1) 4(1). Now if you picked No. 4 you would be right."
Herby took a bite.

"The next question is: Ten minus (-8) = ? The answer is 18. Again the choice is taken from the following: 1(18) 2(-18) 3(2) 4(-2). Here No. 1 would be the correct answer." Herby had some coffee.

Jim put down his coffee cup. "Thanks a lot for solving a couple of problems, Herby."

"That's okay. Anytime I can help I'll be glad to do it." Herby placed a tip under the plate and got ready to tackle the cab job again.

When Jim was back at work he commented to George, "You were right about Herby. He's good at math." Jim scratched his head, and added, "Maybe what I need is some gin," he grinned.

"I thought he would help you," George answered him, " and I can give you some advice. If you want to get ahead on the force, you have to make a lot of pinches — grab the gambler, number writer, pimp, prostitute — that kind. I never did, and maybe that's why I never got anywhere. If you want chevrons, you must play ball with the big shots, Jim".

"Don't misunderstand me, George. I like your advice, but I haven't got the job yet. Maybe things will change soon."

Tests in the town for patrolman were generally given on a Saturday in a public school. On Saturday morning, Jim took the test in West Philly, and when it was over, he went home to eat, then go back to the store.

"How did the test go?" George questioned Jim as he walked in the door.

"The sample questions helped me a lot, and I think I did well, but I won't be sure until I'm notified." Jim sighed and went to work.

CHAPTER 3

It was four months later when Jim got his rating on the Civil Service test. He was qualified for the job. Three months after that, he received a notice to report to the Police Academy on the 21st of the month.

It was a Friday night, and Jim read the letter.

"That will be a week from next Monday," George said.

"Affirmative," Jim answered. He was very pleased.

As Jim would be quitting in a week to go on the force, the manager brought in a new man on Monday, and introduced him to everybody. "Meet Don Ellsman," he announced.

Don was of medium build, slender pointed chin and wore his hair in an unusual manner for a black man. His hair was parted in the middle and a strand brought down toward the eye. Don would be at home in a tuxedo.

Although the Liquor Board had a school for pretraining, there was much more to learn to become a good clerk. The manager took Don over to the register — the same one Joe Clark worked on — to brief Don on procedures.

The manager was speaking, "Don't recommend any brand names. You may suggest types such as Sherry, Port, Muscatel, etc. Now listen as Joe makes a sale."

Joe greeted the customer. "May I help you?"

The customer asked for a pint of whisky, and Joe got the pint, setting it on the counter.

"Anything else?" inquired Joe.

"No, that's all," the patron answered.

Joe said, "Three out of five." He placed the money on the register sill, rang up three dollars and extracted the change from the till. He put the five in the drawer and closed it before going to the buyer.

"Three out of five," he repeated, making the change, then added, "Thank you." That completed the sale.

"If there are any questions about making a sale, don't be afraid to ask me," the manager cautioned. "Now, if a customer claims he gave you a ten and you only handed him change for a five, you call me." Then, "pointing to the top of the register, "I'll take a reading on your key letter. You will then count the money in the till. The proper amount should be the reading I took plus the twenty dollars change you started with. If it is correct, he only gave you a five. If five dollars over he gave you a ten and you'll return the five to him saying you're sorry." The manager glanced in Joe's drawer before he told Don of another step in the procedure.

"As soon as you've collected a hundred dollars over your change, I would like you to bring the money in the office and I'll credit it to you and deposit it in the safe."

"If I'm really busy, can I make an exception?" asked Don.

"I would prefer you wouldn't. Just excuse yourself for a moment and most customers won't mind. If you run into difficulty, just see me. Good luck." The manager shook Don's hand.

"Okay, and thanks." Don started his first day.

A couple of hours later Jim pulled George aside. "Do you notice the way Don walks?"

"How could I miss?" George commented.

A little later George confronted Don, saying, "Your walk impresses me. It reminds me of a military step." He demonstrated with a one-two step to show Don what he had in mind.

"No, it's not a military step. My father taught it to me. He is the originator of the Magnetic Personality Theory. Would you like to see our meeting place? I'll ask Jim and Joe if they would come along."

Jim and Joe were glad to go along, so after they turned in their receipts for the day they all arrived at the Society of Personal Magnetism.

Don went over to the speaker's platform and looked at the audience of three, then spoke, "I told George a few things about the magnetic walk, and I would like to emphasize that anything I know, I learned from my wonderful father."

"Your father must be a good teacher," said George.

"He's great. He's teaching advanced math in Community College now."

"You're lucky having a dad like that," Jim spoke up. Magnetic Diet, Sex Magnetism, the Magnetic Voice and I might have something to say about cholesterol, which seems to be a provocative subject."

"Hit me with that sex magnetism first," George called out. He smacked his lips and added, "I don't want to miss that."

Don drank a glass of water that he had poured from the pitcher on the stand, then directed his gaze with a twinkle of the eye toward George, saying, "I think you're going to be disappointed, George, but because it does not take too long, I can paraphrase."

He looked at the blackboard in back of him, saying, "I won't need that."

"A man must not make a woman just serve him. He should idolize her."

"Ain't that an old-fashioned idea?" challenged George.

"It might be. However, that's what the magnetic method teaches. I'll go on now." Don lifted his eyebrows. "You should quicken her heart, win her good opinion, better everyone of her senses and make her more desirable. Ah . . . you should bring out her natural charms. No caveman stuff, and in turn, the woman should glorify the man."

"I get the idea, Don, but I doubt whether people will comply in these times," George spoke up again.

"Well, George, at times it's necessary to alter one's character to attain the objective," Don revealed.

"I don't want to sound like a dirty old man, but I thought you were going to tell us about aphrodisiacs and that kind of matter." George ran his fingers through his hair.

"When people lead a life embracing the magnetic art, they don't require chemical boosters. Their way of living instills within them an aphrodisiacal quality." Don gave George another twinkling glance.

"To hear the customers in our store you would think we sell all the aphrodisiacs," Joe laughed.

Don shifted his eyes toward Joe. "If they think liquor helps, it's all right with me. To each his own. A drinking habit does not tally with the magnetic personality. However, the hypnotic effect established through the use of alcolol is pleasing to some people. It is documented that too much alcohol in the body can actually place the person in a coma."

Don reached for his brief case, came down from the speaker's stand and stopped near his fellow workers, saying, "I know you would like to see the pictures I brought with me. Aw, here are a few where I hold a goblet of water filled to the brim. The idea is to swing the glass to various positions without spilling a drop. I'm happy to report that I succeeded."

"It looks as though you were wearing pantyhose," Jim said.

"You're absolutely correct, Jim. I was fresh out of my tights. They were at the laundry, so my wife loaned me hers. I think she thought I would have a hard time squeezing into them, but I must tell you they were a perfect fit. My wife said they looked better on me than on her. Oh, the flattery, but fellows, I think I'm graceful enought to look well even in my plain black or white tights, but some of my male friends say I turn them on."

It was Don's first Friday night at the liquor store. The manager watched for about an hour to see that everything went along okay, and when he noticed that Don had no trouble, he tackled the paper work in the office.

"You know Don, every Friday night there has to be something to shake you up. I just hope it's nothing bad," Joe spoke up.

"I second the motion," answered Don.

Jim passed George in the aisle and whispered, "That Don is about as funky as you can get."

"Yeah, but he sure has something to brag about. He really looks good, but I won't say he could turn me on," George declared.

As they approached the counter, two hippies were in their line. One was black, the other white, and both wore very flashy pants. The white hippie had very long hair, and the black dude had an afro.

A black customer in front of the two greeted the white hippie with half a sneer and said, "Hello, Paleface."

"I don't want to be called names," the white hippie growled.

His black friend joined and pointed his finger. "Yeah, man, no names."

George motioned to Don and asked, "Do you think you can apply the personal magnetic theory now?"

"I'll give it a try." Don approached the hippie, and putting on his best charm, said, "What seems to be the trouble?"

"Well, he called me a Paleface, and I think the implication is I don't belong here," answered the white hippie.

Again his friend came to his aid, saying, "Yeah, he's implying too much, man."

Don stepped back a little to give the impression he wouldn't think of fighting, then said, "I certainly feel you mean well, and we should all be cool and considerate. Can you suggest what you would like to be called?" He looked directly at the white hippie.

"Non-black!" was the startling reply.

"Non-black? Wouldn't the implication be more so?" Don asked.

"There was a time when nobody was supposed to call a person black. The foreigners were the only people to use black in describing anyone. The Polish said 'Chorni,' and the Germans used their word for black which is 'Schwarze,' " explained the hippie.

Don directed his next questions to the black customer who had called the hippie 'Paleface.' "Would you think it okay to call him non-black, kind sir?"

With a broad smile, he answered, "Sure, I'll call him that as long as it won't cost me." He then waved to the hippie who had the grievance and emitted, "Hello, non-blacky."

The hippie seemed satisfied with the revised greeting.

A creep walked in to buy a bottle of wine, and he was wearing a large button on his lapel that read, "Chastise judges, not criminals."

"It's stuff like that which makes me glad I'm not on the force," George commented after the creep left. He hastened to add, "but I hope you do well and pick up some chevrons fast."

"Nobody in business would put out a button like that," Jim assured. "He bought one of those kits and made it himself."

"And he's probably hopped up, too. He's the type you'll have to watch when you're a cop. He makes you wish you were a lover instead of a law man." George ran his fingers through his hair.

The following Saturday, George, Jim and Joe said they would be glad to go to the Society Hall so they could acquire some knowledge of the magnetic theory. Don knew he would be talking about vitamins and that Adolph had an interest in the subject, so he picked Adolph up on the way.

The four were seated, and Don stopped at the water cooler to have a drink and refresh his thoughts on the subject matter, then proceeded to the podium.

"Our subject will be the magnetic diet and vitamins. I know that you will be interested," he winked at Adolph, "but I don't think I should mark time on my first point. The number one beverage in the magnetic diet is clear, cool water. Although the use of alcohol is not totally disregarded, it is referred to as a stimulant." Don lifted his pointer to emphasize. "Stimulants are usually labeled abnormal in our literature, and plain food is recommended over rich food."

"Does spicy food rate a no-no?" Joe asked.

"Well, Joe, we advise people who eat in restaurants to order foods that are not highly seasoned. Also, foods with rich gravies should not be considered." Don spoke sincerely.

"How about fruits and vegetables?" George questioned.

"Fruits and vegetables are an accepted, normal part of the diet. Of course, the thing is, don't eat too much."

"The way you're built I can see you don't do that," George remarked.

"I do a lot of exercises, especially the ones that benefit me the most. I'm particularly fond of the one that firms the stomach muscles. I don't have my tights with me, but I can give you the idea." Don looked about the floor for a clean spot.

After sitting, he went back with his head to the floor. Next, he sat up straight, then briskly brought his arms to his feet, touching his toes with his fingers. Next, he laid back again on the floor and repeated the movements.

"You may do this as long as you don't feel uncomfortable," he advised.

"What is the best time to exercise?" asked Jim.

"I spend five minutes in the morning, and five minutes at night just on this one stint."

Since there were no more questions, Don strolled over to the cooler for a drink before continuing his talk.

"Because the vitamin subject is so involved, I would like you to ask questions as we go along."

Adolph put up his hand immediately. "Are vitamins really necessary?" he asked.

"Yes. They're essential in the diet, and all the doctors will agree on that, but they may disagree on the way they should be administered."

"Can we get enough vitamins in our regular diet?" Jim asked.

"The theory is a person would get the required amounts and kinds of vitamins in a well-balanced diet, but in elderly people, who can't chew their food properly, a problem arises. In people who are allergic to certain foods, they also could benefit by a supplement of vitamins. I would have to say that most doctors would suggest a supplement."

"Would I get sick if I didn't take them?" George inquired.

"Well, George, the FDA insists the diet would have to be deficient for a long time before any illness would appear." Don raised the pointer toward the chart. "The FDA also stresses that most tests for vitamin deficiency and its relation to illness were performed on insects and rats, etc., so proof of a corresponding result in the human has not been substantiated."

Joe Clark raised his hand, and asked, "How about pantothenic acid. Does that stop the hair from getting gray?"

"That's a perfect example of what the FDA is talking about. Restoring the hair to the original color by the use of pantothenic acid has never been proven, although some of their tests were successful.

If you want to hear of some more claims about pantothenic acid, Joe, they went like this: Ah, the span of life of fruit flies increased 28%, water insects lived three times as long." Don rolled his eyes toward the ceiling. "And that's not all. The claim went on that the male sex organs of rats gained in size and output. Who is to determine the authenticity?"

"What kind of vitamins are we supposed to take?" George asked. He was immensely interested.

"I'm not a doctor so I wouldn't tell people what to take, but if the doctor prescribes vitamins it's okay. There have been tests with vitamin B12 on humans that have proved highly effective.

"Claims that some vitamins would inhibit cancerous growths have been definitely proven to have no foundation, and the FDA has stopped this propaganda."

Adolph got the attention of Don and asked, "Will vitamins help someone with poor circulation?"

Don raised his chin a little, and answered, "Good question, Adolph. I wish I had an answer, but a person who suffers with poor circulation should consult with his doctor. I had a customer at the store yesterday who asked me if a drink would help. I told him to try a little, and now the same idea can be applied to vitamins — try a little."

Don looked at the clock. It was five p.m. and time to go home. They all stopped at Jack's shack for a beer, before they parted company.

CHAPTER 4

The next Thursday night, Don discovered that some winos were really not dumb. Harry the Horse, so called because he liked to play the horses came up to Don's counter.

"Do you know why the X-ray is so valuable?" Harry asked.

"Why?" said Don, not really interested.

"Because it enabled science to see beneath the surface." Harry was fast with another question. "Do you know why philosophy can't be a science?"

Don shook his head.

"Because the other fellow can agree with you — whether you're right or wrong — just to avoid an argument."

Don agreed, proving Harry the Horse's point.

"Before I go," Harry lifted a finger for emphasis, "I guess you heard about the kids who read poorly. Well, I'm sorry to say I think it's the attitude of the students toward the teacher. No one can learn anything if he uses the same strategy as a guy who could walk into a doctor's office and say, 'Come on, Doc, hurry up and cure me, you s.o.b.' "

Harry didn't wait for an answer, but skipped out with his bottle of apple wine.

Don liked the idea of meeting lots of people, and enjoyed meeting with the members of the Society. Since it was Jim's last week at the store he thought it would be good to get together again and talk about the voice. He called the members, asking them to be at the meeting house at seven p.m.

When they were all seated, George noticed a piano on the speaker's platform. Don explained that it had been there when his father leased the store front years ago. The ivory keys were yellow with age, but no one had played it for a long time.

Don took a nice long drink from the cooler before appearing on the dias. "Gentlemen, I'm going to speak about the voice, but first I'd like to say something that will interest Jim and George.

"There's a whole new can of worms opening up in the study of criminal behaviour. I presume you've heard of some of the experiments." Don pointed to his lapel. "Like pinning a flower on the alleged criminal's lapel. The reaction is noted." Don lifted the pointer he held in his hand. "Too many law violators portray little or no emotion. An interesting angle is now being explored in the field of music."

"Music?" George almost shouted.

"Right. I was about to say the most noted penologist of our time has said, 'There must be a musical tone or chord that can capture the emotion of the most hardened criminal.' " Don waved the pointer.

"I understand there have been experiments with vitamins," Jim proffered.

"True. Some of the convicts were on vitamin programs, but officials rejected the plan. They said that there would be those who would break the law just to obtain vitamin therapy," Don stressed.

Don then asked the fellows whether they would like a refreshing drink of water, and after their thirst was satisfied, George asked, "Do you think that the voice makes a difference when talking to criminals?"

"In most cases I think it does," Don answered. "Talking nice to a criminal won't convert him to a saint, but he'll think the officer of the law is not out just to get him. The main thing is that your voice should be pleasing."

Joe Clark interrupted, "Wouldn't that apply in speaking to anyone?"

Don lifted his gaze as he answered. "Having an attractive voice plus other fine characteristics greatly enhance a person's chances of succeeding. There is probably no business or job in which a person with a pleasing voice cannot benefit," Don added, using the magnetic voice. "A person always emphasizes the right word or words in a sentence to give the correct meaning. Plenty of practice is necessary to attain the round voice in preference to the flat. Growling and snapping should be avoided, and it is very important that the tone not be monotonous. Intelligence is reduced when there is no variation in the tonal scale."

An older member of the society raised his hand and asked, "Does that mean you must sound girlish at times?"

Laughter rang throught the room.

"No, nothing like that. Neither does it mean a girl should give forth with a mannish note. It means the scale has to change — the range must be developed. Practice on the upper range (E as in leak), the middle range (A as in father), and the lower range (O as in row). Just remember to alter the refrain. Don't get stuck on the same thing over and over again.

"A refreshing posture is important in everyday life." Don walked to the cooler to brace his vocal chords. "You must learn how to modify the voice with the lips and at times the cheeks and other parts of the face."

Don strolled to the blackboard directly behind him and placed the pointer on the ledge. Picking up the chalk, he drew the symbol for a loud-speaker on the board.

"I've had some electronic schooling, and I can tell you it's the difference that conveys intelligence. As it stands, there is no sound coming out of this speaker." Don drew the symbol for a coil next. "Now, we apply a direct magnetic current to the voice coil of the speaker. Still no sound from the speaker. We must have a change or difference in the magnetic field before we hear anything, so the signal (desired sound) is superimposed. This signal is an alternating current,"

Don showed the signal on the board by drawing wavy lines. "The alternating current vibrates in the direct magnetic field, and the difference in the two fields duplicates the sound from the original source."

Don replaced the chalk, and added, "I didn't intend to get too technical, but I wanted to explain the importance in proper modulation of the voice."

He glanced at the clock. It was close to nine. "To sum up this segment of my theory I think if you are sincere you can ride smoothly along the conversation road. Your listeners will be grateful for impressive manners and you will gain an eloquent standing in any community,"

"How long should a person spend on the lessons?" Jim asked.

"It takes many weeks of practice before you are on the road to perfection. I'll give each of you a valuable exercise and visual aids, and I wish you all success."

Don drove those that needed a ride home, but Adolph declined his invitation, saying he would rather walk..

It was Saturday and George waited on his first customer, Jerry the Joker. Jerry's greeting was always the same, "Keep a cool head and a warm bosom." Jerry got his nickname from this philosophical quip.

"Herby and Don must have been born under the same star," he said to George. "They are both very suave. You know — suave de faire — I'm lucky to have car fare. That's a joke, son," Jerry curled his tongue toward his nose. "If things were only different when I was a baby, maybe I'd be suave too. I wasn't dropped on my head when I was small, I was bounced up and down." Jerry made a noise that sounded like a sick barn owl.

"Oh yeah!" George agreed.

"Just because you know Ben Gay, don't rub it in, boy!" exclaimed Jerry. He got his bottle of tokay, but before leaving he asked, "Do you like rock music?"

"Not really," George answered.

"You won't guess why I like rock."

"Why?"

"Because it sounds so good when it stops." Jerry laughed, then continued, "To change the subject, George, years ago people who were greatly interested in tea said that there was a substance called theophylline which was good for sick hearts. Do you think the winos think wine is good for the heart?"

"Well, maybe some do. I can tell you that there was a guy who used to buy a half gallon of red wine at least twice a week. He had a hemmorrhage one day and dropped right in front of a hospital, which was lucky for him. When he recovered he said no more red wine — now he drinks white wine."

It was closing time at nine p.m., and after the clerks checked in their cash, everybody gathered in the office. Since Adolph didn't work Saturdays, he took a bus and joined the others to wish Jim farewell and good luck.

Don stepped forward and made the good-bye speech. "We wish you the best, Jim. We'll miss you, but understand you would be pleased to get into a new field. To help you attain success in your chosen task, we are delighted to give you this book."

Don handed Jim a book entitled, *How To Succeed By The Magnetic Method*, autographed by Elwood Ellsman, Don's father.

"Thank you very much, fellows. I'll be thinking of you often. I'll stop in to see you, too, Jim swept his eyes over them.

Everyone shook hands with Jim, and expressed their good wishes in his new employment.

After dinner in the Dallas home, a band consisting of a guitar, bass, drum, and piano played in the living room. Harry was only eighteen, and he had large, expressive eyes, small ears and an afro hairdo. Albert stopped in. He was twenty, and he had wavy hair, small eyes and a rounded chin. There were several girls there — an assortment of young, charming black and Puerto Rican darlings who were either intrigued by the music or Larry. The father wasn't crazy about country music, so he wasn't in the room. There was a little girl who killed Albert inwardly. She played the piano, and her every movement made a hit with Albert. It was beauty coupled with grace that intrigued him. She seemed to exert no effort in running her fingers across the keyboard. Albert thought she would make a good surgeon.

Her eyes were always on Larry. Why wouldn't she give him a tumble? Maybe she was afraid to be off tune if she didn't look at Larry. Albert listened to some country music then went into the dining room for some pre-med study.

His father was there. "What's the matter, Albert? Don't you like country music?"

"I like it, but I have to study now."

"How about all those nice girls. Don't they send you?"

"Flora, the piano player, certainly does, but she won't notice me," Albert said.

"That's what you think, Albert. When I was in the living room I saw her sneaking glances at you. Maybe she knows you have to study. Don't forget, she also has to watch the musicians to keep in tune."

"You really think so Dad?" Albert thought for a while before going upstairs.

George got up from the chair to go to the room that was referred to as "the room way back." Three years earlier when Mrs. Dallas became ill, George had enlarged the shed to three times its original size. It became the room where Mrs. Dallas would be taken care of. She did not want to go to a hospital even if her husband had been able to pay the bill. George, who worked three days and three nights at the liquor store, did not talk about his sick wife at the store.

Rose Quinn who lived next door and took care of Mama Dallas when George was working, had gone home. She was short of stature, the motherly type. She was just wonderful in caring for Mary. She knew George had no money to hire a nurse. Rose lived with her sister-in-law who was a widow. The widow took care of their house, so Rose was glad to help the Dallas household.

The room was packed with two beds, a portable toilet and other things to help care for her. The cabinet contained pills, heart medicine, water pills, high blood pressure pills and also vitamins. George was to see that Mary got the prescribed diet.

"How do you feel, Mary?" George asked softly.

Mary smiled — a beautiful smile. Her cheeks were slightly hollow and her eyes a little sunken. The doctor had not put it on the line — had not told George of the seriousness of her heart condition.

"I'm all right, how are the boys?"

"They're fine. Nothing to worry about, Mary." He kissed his wife good night. He had to work the early shift the next day.

Late one evening, Don met Adolph in an aisle in the back of the store. Adolph was sweeping and stopped when he saw Don.

"Would you know anybody who needs a room?" Adolph asked.

"Are you looking for a white tenant?" asked Don.

"If the person is okay, it's all right. My Puerto Rican tenant was great, but he got married and has his own place now."

"I'll see what I can do for you, Adolph."

It was only two hours later when Sergio Gonzales asked Don whether he knew anyone who had a vacant room. The Puerto Rican said his nephew needed a room.

Don called out to Adolph, and Adolph spoke to Mr. Gonzales. "All right, Mr. Gonzales. Tell your nephew to come around and look it over." Adolph marked down the address on a piece of paper. "If he'll come over Sunday, I'll be in," he advised.

"My nephew's name is Carlos — Carlos Gonzales."

"Right, I hope he likes the room," Adolph added.

Adolph opened the door in answer to Carlos's ring. Carlos Gonzales was good looking with his mustache and long, black wavy hair. He was wearing a black and white checkered jacket.

"Hello," Carlos spoke up. "Mr. Teitleman, my uncle sent me to look at the room you have."

"Whoa. Don't call me that. Everybody calls me Adolph."

"Okay, Adolph. I'll remember that," Carlos promised.

"Let's go upstairs, Carlos."

As they entered the room, Carlos whistled. "Four windows. Cool man, cool."

"You like that, eh?" asked Adolph. "Only house on West Pearl Street with four windows in the back room."

"Yeah, here's why I like it." Carlos took a little booklet out of his jacket and asked Adolph to watch. "I draw all the cartoons then fasten them together. See — I'll riffle them and you'll notice the action."

Adolph saw a continuous action in animated sequence. "Boy, that's great," he commented.

"I'll have plenty of light to see what I'm drawing," Carlos said.

"Say, Carlos, you don't happen to know Don who works in the store, do you?"

"I don't go in the store very much, Adolph, so I can't say I know him."

"I'm sure he'd be interested in your talent for drawing. He has a theory called Magnetic Personality, and he probably would be glad to have you make the illustrations."

"Fine, tell him I'll be glad to help."

"I'll see Don tomorrow, then let you know when you can meet him. How soon would you like to move in?"

"I'd like to move in Saturday, but I can meet Don any time."

"Yeah. If you need a radio I can let you have one because I have three," Adolph offered.

"Thank you for your kindness. Here's a week's rent, Adolph." Carlos counted out the fifteen bucks.

Adolph gave the young artist the key, saying, "Now don't lose it,

Carlos."

"Don't worry about me. I never get drunk and I won't bring in any trouble-makers. No girls either," Carlos winked.

Adolph met Don the next Monday afternoon. "I've got a new roomer, Don. He's great at drawing cartoons and he can make them move. I might have rushed it, but I told him you would be interested. Did I do wrong?"

"No, I guess I could have a chat with him. Did you tell him where we may meet?" asked Don.

"Not yet, but I thought William's would be convenient to both of you. He works part-time, however."

"Tell him that I'll be able to see him at six tomorrow."

On Tuesday, Susie waited on the two at William's. Carlos ordered a fish filet and french fries, and Don had fruit salad and black coffee.

Don was fascinated with the little movie Carlos showed him. It depicted a couple of flying trapeze artists at work.

"Beautiful, just beautiful, Carlos. You capture every detail in movement."

"The gritty guys used to keep me moving on my seat. The circus was the only place I ever went to with my father," Carlos informed between mouthfuls. "My parents divorced when I was only eight years old."

"How old are you now?" asked Don.

"I'm twenty-one. My mother died when I was ten, and I've never seen my father since the divorce. I went to live with my uncle, but to get back to the man on the trapeze, I got the feeling I would like to see one of the acrobats close up and talk to him." Carlos scooped up some french fries. "Would you care for some fries?" he asked.

"No thank you," said Don. "I like them, but I want to stay shapely." He pulled in his stomach.

"When I was about eleven, I tried to see the performer at the circus, but didn't make it until a year later. I told one of the guys that I had a composition to do on a trapeze act and I saw Galona, the wonderful aerial artist . . . ." Carlos bent forward in his chair and his eyes lit up. "When I got home, I took my crayons and started to draw Galona. I had memorized every inch of his superb body," exclaimed Carlos.

"You really have a talent, Carlos. Did you ever think of making money from it?" Don boosted the coffee to his lips.

"I'm working part-time in illustrating advertising." Carlos gave a meaningful sweep of the hand. "You could say I'm at the bottom. No connections, you know."

"I'm the president of the Society of Personal Magnetism, Carlos. We meet at 4th and Girard. I'll send you a card and if you wish, you can attend our meetings."

"I'd be happy to do so. Maybe I'll learn how to succeed." Carlos was overjoyed.

"I'm sure you'll gain some knowledge. I'm thinking of writing a book on my magnetic exercises, and perhaps you could do the illustrating." Don handed Carlos a card. "Jot down your phone number for me, please."

"I'll only be at my uncle's this week, then I'll be living at Adolph's place."

"Oh, that's right. Then you don't have to give me the number. I already have Adolph's. We're going to have an important meeting on Thursday at seven. Try to be there, if you can. I'll look forward to see-ing you there."

Jim stopped in on Wednesday and asked George to meet him at William's for lunch.

They ordered their dinner and George looked at Jim. "What hap-pened?" he asked.

"Just that I've been promoted to detective and thought you'd like to know," said Jim with a smile on his face.

"Yeah. You made it fast. Are you sure you don't know somebody." George drank the stimulant.

"The one thousand plus is a big help," Jim announced.

"The real money . . . the real money is made by the captain, inspector and of course the director and deputy." George recounted.

"It's a long climb to commissioner," Jim added.

"The way you're going, Jim, I think you'll make it. When are you going to get another promtion?"

"Pretty soon, I hope. How is Don?"

George refreshed with another swallow of coffee, then continued. "He's okay. He 's getting ready to give us the run-down on cholesterol tomorrow. Will you be able to come?"

"What time is the meeting?" Jim finished his beverage.

"At seven."

"Tell Don I'll be there. I don't want to miss that important meet-ing."

"I sure will," George promised. They were both ready to return to work.

CHAPTER 5

Jim, Adolph, Larry, Carlos and the girls all came on Thursday night to the hall. Also, six of the real old-timers were present.

Don spoke from the rostrum. "We have some new listeners tonight so I'd like to open by saying, 'Electricity can startle a dead frog as well as a live one. We need a human to make us vital — to guide us — to drive away nervousness.' "

"There is so much to talk about cholesterol that I would like to have questions asked by you. Who would like to be first?"

"Is cholesterol a new subject?" Carlos asked.

"Definitely not," Don lowered his eyes to the notes. "Blood cholesterol, referred to as a bile solid, was first found in the gall bladder in 1769 by a Frenchman. May I have another question?"

Adolph appeared embarrassed, but asked, "What about eggs?"

"That's an important question and I expected someone to bring it up. A great deal of confusion exists concerning eggs, and it is no secret that some doctors have told their patients to cut down on them. There are reports, however, that eggs contain lecithin which is supposed to lower the cholesterol level, therefore, it is all right to eat them. No conclusive evidence has been reached as yet."

"Are all people susceptible to high levels of cholesterol?" Jim questioned.

"No, Jim. There are persons blessed with blood vessels through which cholesterol passes without any harm. It is when the substance gets stuck in the vessels in quantity that the trouble starts. Levels above 240 are in the danger zone.

"What kind of diet is recommended?" George asked.

Don walked back from the cooler, and answered, "Here again there is a difference in the suggestions of doctors. One doctor will say to eat normal servings of meat, but stay off the sugars. He allows 500 calories of carbohydrates a day. This is equal to eight slices of bread, or four medium potatoes. This could be bad for a person who tolerates carbohydrates poorly. He or she would have a craving for more carbohydrates to make up calories and aggravate the condition."

Don looked over his notes again. "I must tell you what the doctor who commends a low meat diet allows. It is four or five servings of fish a week and lots of vegetables."

"Should everybody try to lower their cholesterol level?" One of the girls questioned.

Don chuckled. "For a while I thought the girls couldn't talk, but to answer you, experts say that people who should give thought to lowering their cholesterol input are those that are obese, persons who have had a coronary, apoplexy, or the unfortunate ones who have had relatives afflicted with hardening of the arteries. These people seem to be vulnerable to cholesterol deposits on the artery wall.

"If there are no more questions, "I'll lock up and anyone needing a ride home can meet me outside. Thank you all for coming."

It was early on Saturday and Jerry the Joker hung over the counter, saying to George, "Hey, you know what Confucius says?"

"What does he say, Jerry?" said George.

"He says, 'He who makes love in park has peace on earth.' "

"How about that. I didn't know that," commented George.

"Yeah. I'll throw one more in before I take my bottle home. That guy in the park was in a state of eufiveia. Get it? That's one more than euphoria."

George smiled. "Yeah, I get it. See you later."

Jim Smith stopped by the store and asked George to meet him at William's for lunch.

Over coffee, Jim said, "You don't have any daughters so you don't have the worry of their getting mugged on the street, George. Well, I guess you heard of the two blocks in town where all the gays live?"

"You mean around Elm and Spruce?" asked George, enjoying his coffee.

"Right. Curiously enough, those two blocks are the safest place for a girl to walk, work, or even live."

"I can understand that. The gays are not interested in girls," George agreed.

"I made a pinch the other day which was a spin-off of the gay thing. Two guys were in a tap room, and one fellow says to the other, 'I'll bet you ten bucks you ain't got the nerve to call the first truck driver you see coming down the street a gay.' The guy ran out to the street and did call the first truck driver he saw a gay. He won the bet all right, but I had to take him to the hospital. I also busted the truck driver."

"Well, that's a pinch to your credit." said George, taking a bite of his sandwich.

Jim took a bite out of the grilled cheese. "Yeah, George. How's Don? I really miss him. I guess he'll have something going today."

"Not at the hall, Jim. He's going to meet Carlos, you know the Puerto-Rican fellow who was sitting next to Larry in the last meeting. Carlos is good at drawing cartoons, and tonight they're going to discuss illustrating a book of exercises that Don is writing."

They finished their lunch, then headed for the revolving door. Jim took the seat of his cruiser and George went back to the store.

Don and Carlos started to work on the pictures that evening.

"I have all my notes and everything here so I thought we would begin the job in my parlor," Don said.

"Any place will be all right with me. I like to prove that I can draw." Carlos lifted his eyebrows.

"Well, you've already proven that to me with those wonderful trapeze pictures. They really move," praised Don.

"Thank you, Don."

"I'm going to start our project with the calisthenics that are helpful to people with arthritis of the feet," Don began. He removed a folder from the desk and opened it to the proper spot. "You'll notice five poses here. In the first, the man is holding his knees in a stiff position. He has each hand on a chair or such support, and in the next picture he swings up on his toes. In the next the swing is back on the heels. In the following two sketches, the movement is back on the heels then on the toes. You see it is an alternating action, first rising on the toes then putting the weight on the heels. It should not be done for more than thirty times. If you could show a continuous action as you did with the aerial performers, I could get the booklets duplicated and they would be given to the buyers of the book."

"This will be easy compared to the trapeze job," Carlos admitted, then added, "I'll get my thin magic marker and start right away on it."

"Leave part of the larger pictures blank for the instructions," Don explained.

Carlos had the individual pictures completed in two hours.

"Beautiful, just magnificient," Don said, admiring the drawings.

"When I take these home, I'll work on the booklet in my spare time," Carlos promised.

"We'll be busy on some other exercises in about a week, but before you leave, I'd like to say I think you are the type of young man who is willing to help others provided it works no hardship on yourself. You're definitely not the kind that seeks information without giving it. That kind should be avoided. If a man is unwilling to cooperate, then he shouldn't be given helpful information.

"One should always be glad to give a favor when he knows it will be returned, and the desire to meet a man halfway will keep things cool. It's probably another way of saying that it does not harm a person to be open-minded. Above all, do not take the attitude that the sole mission in life is to pump someone. Truly, I'm not saying you give me that impression. In fact, you give me the opposite image."

Carlos wished Don good night.

It was two week later when Don called Carlos and asked him to stop over. "We'll do the other group of pictures, if it's okay with you, Carlos," Don suggested.

Carlos had very few hang-ups, but he had never kicked the strange habit of snooping. It began when he was ten years old when he lived with his aunt and uncle next to a mansion that belongs to a very wealthy family. The mansion had been vacant for quite some time. Carlos would climb over the low fence into the yard to where two large pear trees stood. Carlos plucked pears many times and his aunt made sauce and preserves from them. One day after he had picked a few pears, he noticed a window leading to the basement was open. He lowered himself into the cellar and saw some empty wooden cases that had contained Scotch whisky. The aroma from these cases was unique, and in one of the boxes he found twenty-five Indian head pennies. He still had those pennies.

Now the urge to snoop grabbed Carlos again. He entered Adolph's room, glanced about, and saw a large diary on the dresser. Quietly, he looked at some of the entries. Then he found a letter between the pages. It was addressed to Adolph and was signed, "Your loving niece, Jeanne." Carlos read the romantic love letter, then quickly returned it to its place in the diary. He then went back to his room and prepared for his meeting with Don.

Carlos arrived at Don's place on time, and Don wasted no time in getting started.

"Carlos, I'm going ahead with the exercises that are beneficial in a sore back condition. This is a common ailment, and I think people will be glad to get relief. I have six stills on this, but of course you'il need more for the animation.

"This is a great exercise to do just before breakfast. Number one is to start with the feet about twenty inches apart, keeping the knees rigid. Number two is to put your arms toward the ceiling with the neck all the way back. Number three is to move the trunk down slowly, bringing the arms down easily until they are on a line with the floor. Don't go down to the floor on the first attempt, but touch the floor on the third try, each time going lower until the palms of the hands touch the floor. Number four, go back to the starting position each time, and number five, before trying to touch the floor with the palm of your hand, just go as far as you can. Finally, number six, with the open hand touch the floor. When you can feel the floor with the back part of the palm, you're doing fine. The beginner does this as many times as possible without getting tired. Twenty to thirty times is average, and if done three times a day, the kinks ought to come out of the vertebra. A person in ill health, however, should consult his doctor before trying this exercise.

"Do you think you have the idea from these pictures, Carlos?"

"I don't think I'll have any trouble. I'll make more movements of the trunk as it goes toward the floor."

"Remember, leave one half of the paper blank. I'll need it for the directions. If the book sells, I'll see that you are rewarded."

"Forget it, Don, I'm not looking for a reward. I just want to keep on drawing so I won't get stale," explained Carlos.

On Wednesday at the liquor store a guy pushed in front of Jerry the Joker to get a bottle. Jerry let him go ahead, and after the pusher left, Jerry said, "That guy thinks arrogance is a coat of polish. If there is anything he lacks it is polish. How are you doing, George?"

"All right, but my wife is sick. I don't mind paying the doctor and buying the medicine, but she's not getting better."

"Why don't you get a white card?" Jerry asked.

"White card? What's that?"

"You get the card when you go on welfare. They pay for everything — doctors, medicines, operations and whatever you need. I should know. My wife is sick and welfare pays," Jerry informed.

"Well, I can't give up my job to go on welfare," George sighed.

"I think I told you before that I have a heart condition and had to get welfare, but next year I'll be old enough to be on medicare. Welfare will then pay for the part that medicare doesn't. Well, George, I hope your wife gets better soon."

"Thanks," George answered and handed the bagged bottle to Jerry.

George was thinking about his debts when Nick Gross came into the store. Nick worked for a finance company where George had made a loan five years earlier, and occasionally they would have a beer together. Nick was black, 180 lbs., five feet, nine inches, and about forty years old.

"You're just the man I want to see," hailed George.

"Money, I'll bet," Nick answered, removing the cigar from his mouth.

"What else? Don't tell me they are fresh out?"

"No . . . as long as you don't want a million," Nick smiled.

"I'll be off Friday night. I know your office won't be open, so can I stop by your house?"

"For a friend, sure, George. Don't eat too much for we may get a couple of beers. How's the wife?"

George shook his head. "Not very well, Nick. She's been on medication for nine years and she's fed up."

"I know how it is, George. I recall that my mother used to hate to take medicine. Well George, I'll take my bottle of gin and see you later."

On Friday, George told his wife, Mary, that he was going to borrow some money. "I'm seeing Nick Gross tonight to fill out the papers. Rose, bless her, will be here to stay with you, so don't worry, Mary."

After Nick and George got together, Nick started to ask the necessary questions. "How old are you, George?"

"I can't keep you guessing, Nick, because it's one of the questions on the papers. I'm fifty-seven and Mary is five years older."

"Does Mary have a heart condition?"

"Yes. The doctor is no stranger in my house," George said sadly.

"One more signature ought to do it." Nick pointed to the line to be signed. "Now you should get the check in a week, George. I feel like a beer, don't you? I'm treating."

They got into Nick's car and rode over to Tom's Cafe, which was Nick's favorite spot.

"You can take your pick here," Nick said with a tap on George's ribs.

There were all kinds of high bouncing ladies — blacks, whites, Chinese, and Puerto Rican — present.

George had just gotten his pay check, but he couldn't afford to peel much from the pile of cash.

"How about the cost?" asked George.

"Don't let that stop you. Your homework hasn't kept you busy?"

"If you mean sex, I've had to forget about it. My wife's been too sick for nine years," George recounted.

Nick reflected for a moment then answered. "Look, George, I know the boss and if you run short I can help. So, don't fret if you find something you can go for."

The beer was making George feel good to the point where he was forgetting his worries.

Nick leaned over and spoke quietly. "When I see a certain chick, I'll bring her over to this table, then I'll move to another. I see somebody I know."

Nick got up when she came it. He immediately decided she was for George. He talked to her for a few minutes then brought her to the company of George.

"Meet Violet," Nick introduced, giving George the look as though heaven was near. He then walked directly to his date at another table.

Violet was a tall long-legged black beauty. She sat close to George — really close, and what a set of knees. The texture, structure and contour was alluring.

"George," she said, "a nice name."

George felt those healthy legs rubbing against his. "Not as pretty as Violet though," he answered. "What do you like to drink?"

"I'll take a beer." Violet squeezed closer saying, "You know, we can play the hidden bone game." She laughed.

George thought it funny that she started off with a bang. He looked across the room to see Nick sitting with a gorgeous Puerto Rican girl.

Violet had only drunk half of her beer when she arose, saying, "I'm going to the ladies room."

George looked at the half full glass of beer and wondered why she was inconvenienced so soon. He went for his wallet in his back pocket, but it wasn't there. Jumping up from his chair, he grabbed Violet before she got to the toilet. He spun her around, snatching her handbag. He opened it and found his wallet. Giving Violet a couple hard slaps on the face, he counted the money and found nothing missing. "I caught you before you could put the bundle you know where," he shouted at her.

"What's going on?" Nick leaped from his place alongside his girl.

Everyone looked on as George gave long legs another blow across her face.

"You mentioned good clean fun, Nick, but you didn't know she was a thief. She stole my wallet, but I got it back. I'm glad I had nothing to do with this crook." He gave her another crack, then ordered a beer.

"This guy wants to kill me. Call the cops," Violet pleaded.

The bar attendant ignored George's request and picked up the phone.

In just a few minutes Jim Smith entered the bar, showing his badge.

"Gee, this is sure fast service," the bartender said.

"What do you mean?" Jim questioned.

"Ain't you answering a call?"

"No. I came in to see George Dallas." Jim pointed to George.

"He's in the middle of the trouble," said the barman.

After hearing the story, Jim couldn't believe that George recovered his money so quickly.

Violet was still screaming for the cops to lock up George. She had the nerve to call for revenge.

Jack Slaton, who had a connection with the dope traffic, was drinking all by himself, but he stood on his feet and spoke loudly, "You ought to lock up the broad. She's nothing but a low-down crook."

"Look who's talking, you creep," she shouted back. "You got me for twenty in New York. I was crazy for investing in that dumb, dumb thing of yours!"

Jack Slaton didn't walk out — he ran as fast as he could. Just then three cops burst into the tavern. The police listened to the story, then Jim walked over to one of them and whispered in his ear. The cop nodded with an expression that he understood.

Jim then went and talked with Violet in an attempt to stop the noise. She was very surprised when she learned why Jim wanted to talk with George. She turned quickly on her patent leather heels and disappeared.

Jim walked over to George, and said, "Let's go outside, George."

Under the green and white awning at the entrance, Jim said, "I don't know whether you saw me whispering, but you'll have to brace yourself George. I can't whisper to you. I have the sad job of telling you that your wife died."

"Oh no." George grabbed the sides of his head.

"I know you feel rotten, George, but there's nothing you can do to help her now. Rose Quinn called the emergency wagon. A buddy of mine was assigned to the wagon and he told me your wife passed away. I called the house and was told you went to meet Nick. I know Tom's Cafe is his favorite spot, so I came here. I'm sorry to bring you such bad news, George. Can I drive you home?"

George didn't answer immediately. He thought of Mary — Poor Butterfly. Stunned, he got into the car with one hand still on his forehead.

When George entered the back room, Mrs. Quinn was fixing things. "I was reading the paper and Mary seemed to be resting. She suddenly sat up, called out your name and then fell back on the pillow. I didn't like the way she looked, so I called the emergency number. The police gave her oxygen, but it didn't help." Rose could hardly speak.

The funeral procession arrived at the family plot in North Cedars Cemetery on the third Tuesday of May. After the final prayer was said, George placed a few flowers on the casket, then patted it. The branches of a small tree from the adjoining grave hung over the Dallas plot. George was lost in emotion when he recalled the second line, 'Neath the blossoms waiting.'

Before leaving, Nick Gross gave George his hand, saying, "I'm sorry for what happened. I had no idea . . . ." Nick did not know how to finish his sentence.

"It wasn't your fault, Nick. I can only blame myself. Thank you for coming, and don't feel guilty. I'll see you later."

CHAPTER 6

It was vacation time for Don, and he thought of his promise to see Max Miller about some exercises. He went to the phone and called Max. "Hello, Max. I wonder if you can give me the phone number of your doctor. I'll have to call him and tell him that I'm going to perform some exercises on your feet."

"Sure, Don. The number is CE5-2500. Are you coming over?"

"Yes, just as soon as the doctor okays it. Probably within the hour.

The doctor had no objection to the therapy that Don would do, so Don was on his way to see Miller. He passed Ben Franklin High School, and in the side yard were a few benches. Juan Orlando was sitting on one of them. He seemed to be entertaining himself — maybe he was, but the slow beat on his bongo drum meant that he had some stuff available. Fast time on the drum meant he needed some from his wholesaler, Jack Slaton. He had no reason to advertise, as business was done by word of mouth. The customer would pass Juan on a slow gait, and Juan would simply say the time, and then the sale of the dope would be made in an empty house about three blocks north of Spring Street.

Don reached 1515 Spring Street, and Miller opened the door.

"Meet my sister, Edna Evans," said Miller with a smile.

"Glad to know you," said Don. "I'm sorry I couldn't bring Lois around, but I told your brother she'll be here . . . let me see, maybe Friday. Okay?"

"That will be fine." Mrs. Evans had gray hair, a round face and a few hairs on her chin. A flowered apron hugged her leisure dress. "Would you care for a cup of coffee or tea?" she asked.

"No thanks, nothing right now," Don answered.

"Now, Max if you'll just sit here." Don placed the hassock in front of Miller's chair. He then lifted Max's foot to the support and worked on Miller's toes.

"See . . . there's nothing to it. I'm drawing your toes upward and then moving them firmly downward. This flexing action will improve the circulation and you should be able to walk better after a few weeks of these exercises." Don continued to work on the toes for about fifteen minutes. He then talked to Miller on the porch before leaving.

"How long has the house next door been vacant?"

"I'd say about four years. There's a young man who goes in and out, and sometimes he carries bundles of old newspapers. His name is Juan, and he told me he waits until he gets enough papers to sell, then he donates the money for the poor kids in the neighborhood. I like him for that, and just the other day I saw him take in a radio, a couple of chairs and a percolator. Some time ago he told me his friend bought the house very cheaply on a sheriff's sale."

"There are plenty of sales these days. See you in a couple of days — take care."

It was Wednesday and Don wanted a quick snack for his lunch. On his way to William's lunch shop, he met Bill Burk, a clerk who had transferred to the store a month earlier. He was white, twenty-five and had small ears and thin lips. He had that far-away stare in his eyes, and wore a two-tone bow tie with a contrasting shirt.

After the waitress took their order, Bill was ready to talk.

"Don, I lost my girl friend. She meant everything to me, and then this guy," Bill turned the grilled cheese over as though examining it, then continued, "This guy who's big in the dope racket got next to her."

"Does she know he's in the dope business?" Don questioned.

"Yes. She knows. Maybe she's satisfied because she can get a fix very easily. I don't know whether she really loves the guy or not."

"If she loves the man, it's hard to say what can be done," Don agreed.

"There's more to it. The girl just happens to be the Police Commissioner's daughter!"

"Her father doesn't know she has this man for a friend, does he?" asked Don.

"I don't think so. He sure wouldn't think of having a son-in-law who is in dope. It would ruin him," Bill answered.

"It's one difficult problem," agreed Don.

"Yeah, and I wouldn't be surprised if he's under the impression that he will get protection from the commissioner." Bill took a drink of coffee.

"Oh, that's the way it is," said Don tasting his drink.

"Yeah, he showers her with gifts and money. That's more that I could do," Bill lamented. "You know, Don, I'm thinking seriously of ratting on the guy."

"I really don't know how to advise you, Bill, but I suppose your own judgment would be best," said Don.

"By the way, Don. How are you enjoying your vacation?"

"It's just started, but I'm doing all right. I'm helping Mr. Miller get on his feet again after he suffered that stroke. I think he'll be able to walk without a cane soon."

"Well, I'm glad we met and had a chat," Bill said, getting up to leave.

"No trouble, Bill. Tell the fellows I asked about them. I've got to get back home."

Don was deep in mental exercises as his car moved toward his apartment.

Don visited Miller on Friday to give him the second round of therapy. This time he brought his wife and daughter along.

Lois was six. Her hair was in a pony tail and she had a dimple in her cheek. Mrs. Evans made a stir about her.

"She is adorable," she said.

"Yes," Max agreed. "Everybody would have to love her."

After the treatment was finalized, the Ellsmans prepared to leave.

"Mrs. Evans," Vivienne Ellsman said, "We'll be glad to have you babysit for Lois if you don't mind."

"I'd be happy to do it," Mrs. Evans said, joyfully.

"I'll see you next week," Don said to Mr. Miller. "It won't be long before you can throw away your cane."

Nearly a year later on a Saturday night in June, Larry talked to his dad. "The concert is just a week from today. Is it all right for me to go, Dad?"

"Are you going by train?" asked George.

"I'd like to go in a car. It's more fun. You can stop when and where you want," said Larry.

"I won't allow you to take our old car all the way down there. The car is not in good condition," explained George.

"I'm not going with our car, Dad. Bill Lambert is going and he told me he had room. I'm talking to him again to be sure," said Larry.

"How old is the car?" asked George.

"It's only two years old, Dad."

"It should be O.K. I just hope Bill is a careful driver, Larry."

"He's a good driver, Dad."

Two of the fellows who were supposed to ride in Bill's car would get a ride in another car so there was plenty of room.

Larry and his friend never reached Nashville. They were riding along a road in Middlesboro, Kentucky, when their car was struck by another auto at an intersection. The other car was operated by a drunken driver who was the only person not killed in the accident.

It had been only a little over a year since George arranged the funeral for his wife.

Again Don lent a helping hand. He went along with George to Middleboro to make arrangements to bring Larry back to Philadelphia. He got the O.K. from his manager to take the time off.

Don also suggested that the guitar that Larry played so well be placed in the grave with him.

It was the most difficult for Alice to say good-bye to Larry, through her tears, for she loved him so.

After Larry's death, nothing went right. George and his son couldn't cut it any more. They went to pieces. George became a helpless drunk. He was chased home by the manger of the store several times when he reported for work in a loaded condition.

Albert tried alcohol, forgetting all about his studies. But alcohol was only a temporary crutch. He graduated to dope. His father was unaware of Albert's habit. Albert had a college friend who was cousin to Juan Orlando, dope agent, punk. The cousin introduced Albert to Juan, a well known hippie who had an uncanny way of keeping his operation secret. If you bought from him, he would remind you, "If you tell there won't be any more of you around."

Don was at his desk working on his book one sticky hot evening in August. Lois was over at Mrs. Evans while her mother had a hair appointment. Don looked out the window and it reminded him to go get his little girl at the Miller house.

Stepping briskly on the porch, he rang the doorbell. He heard something so he put his ear to the door. The cries of Miller were discernible. He broke the glass of the window and stepped into the living room after hearing the scream of his daughter coming from a closet under the stairway. He let Mrs. Evans and Lois out, telling them to run upstairs.

It was a one-sided fight. Juan was beating Miller with no mercy, and Miller fell as Don approached.

Don caught Juan off balance and Juan slipped to the floor, but it was only a momentary gain for when Juan got up, Don realized the fight was an equal match. Both men were of the same height, weight, and stamina. They punched each other as though they were hitting a punching bag. They fought fiercely as they rolled along the floor toward the back of the house. When they reached the kitchen, Juan opened the door, and they continued to poke and pounce upon each other in the yard. By this time they were almost exhausted, and neither could strike a wicked blow. Juan finally fell, and Don dragged him, took out the scotch tape from his pocket that he had placed there just before leaving his house, and wound up the wrists of Juan. Juan was breathing heavily and could not resist. Don also twirled the tape around Juan's ankles, then went to a phone and called the police.

Don then went to Miller's side and said, "You've got a few cuts, but they'll fix you up. What brought all this on, Max?"

"I was speaking to a young man who came out of the house next door, and I asked him if he knew that Juan sold old papers to help the poor kids. He said he didn't know that, and then I asked him whether Juan was working. He never got a chance to answer because Juan appeared suddenly and told him to keep moving. Juan then grabbed me and pushed me inside. He locked my sister and Lois in the closet, and told me if I didn't stop talking, the little girl would disappear. The guy must be doing something wrong, and all along I thought he was a nice fellow." Miller had to pause several times to catch his breath.

"The man must be crazy, Max."

The cops finally arrived and one inquired, "What happened?"

"He tried to kill Miller, I think," Don replied.

"And only because I asked a guy who I thought was his friend whether he had a job," Miller spoke up.

"Will you appear at the hearing, Mr. Miller?" one of the cops asked.

"Yes. I'll be there," Miller promised.

The cop put the cuffs on Juan, saying, "The scotch tape is still holding." He then led Juan to the police car.

Within a few hours Juan was released on bail on a charge of assault and battery.

It was in a pool room that Carlos met Juan. Juan wasn't pushing dope in there — he just wanted to play a game.

"Where's the old man?" asked Juan, meaning Adolph.

"He was too tired to play pool," Carlos answered.

Carlos knew that Juan was rated as a very good player, and was happy because he was winning. Carlos talked to Juan about the love letter that Adolph received from his niece, and Juan acted as if he were very interested.

"Does he ever take her anywhere?" Juan asked.

"Yes. He takes her out sometimes." This made Carlos feel a little uneasy.

"Was she ever married?" questioned Juan.

"Her husband was killed in the Korean War." Carlos wished there would be no more questions.

"Korea?"

"Yes," Carlos returned.

"Look, I have to run now. See you later."

Adolph and his niece were walking home from the 21 Bar two nights later. The area was very dark.

Juan Orlando came out of a store entrance. He had fixed himself a main liner from a new batch, and looked weird with his beard and flowing hair. Juan had seen Adolph in the pool room and at the liquor store. Carlos had given Juan the name of the niece, so Juan started an unwelcomed conversation.

"Nice evening, Adolph," then assuming the lady to be the niece, he asked, "How are you, Jeanne?"

Jeanne was very frightened, but answered, "All right."

Juan figured if Jeanne went for her uncle, she wouldn't turn him down.

"We're going home and would appreciate it if you would let us alone," Adolph spoke up rather firmly.

Juan had no intention of going away, and he showed Adolph a knife. "If you don't interfere with me, you'll stay alive," he warned Adolph.

"I'll give you anything you want, but please leave her alone. Here, take my wallet," Adolph pleaded.

Juan took the wallet, asking, "How much is is there?"

"About fifty dollars," said Adolph, worrying about the look in Juan's eyes.

Jeanne expected more trouble, and looked about for a police car. "Please have my purse," she offered.

Juan kept Adolph's wallet, but paid no attention to Jeanne's purse. He took hold of Jeanne's arm, saying in a gruff voice, "We're going to have a good time." He then smiled.

Adolph lunged at Juan, shouting, "Leave us alone or I'll scream murder."

"I don't like your attitude," Juan said as he stabbed Adolph in the side.

Adolph sank to the ground with a groan.

Juan grabbed Jeanne's arm, saying, "Let's go. I don't want to hurt you." The heroin was taking effect on him.

"You can't leave him here to die," Jeanne pleaded, trying not to panic.

"He'll be all right. I'll call for help up the street." He lied, but kept pulling Jeanne along with him.

"There are so many pretty Puerto Rican girls who would appeal to you, so why are you picking on me?"

Juan wasn't listening. He pulled steadily on her arm until they reached the empty house with an evil drive. He had no opposition now for the fix he had cooked up and needled into his vein.

Jeanne had somehow managed to get off the floor where Juan had pushed her. She managed to kick Juan in the groin.

A look of diabolic hatred swept across Juan's face. "You made the biggest mistake of your life sweetie." He threw her down again, took off her shoe and forced it into her body. She cried out in excruciating pain.

Mr. Miller was out on his porch and heard the horrible scream coming from the house next door. "Did you hear that?" he asked his sister.

"Did I? It was horrible — like somebody getting killed," said Edna, alarmed.

I'm going to call the police." He hurried back into the house and dialed the number.

It was Jim Smith who answered the call and Miller pointed to the house and explained what he had heard.

Jim ran into the house, and what he saw made him wish he had had only a graveyard stew for dinner. He placed the shoe belonging to Jeanne in a plastic bag, then returned to his car and called for an ambulance. When he returned to the house he saw Juan running up to the second floor. Jim chased him, but Juan opened the window and dropped to the shed below. Jim had permission to use the spray gun that would stop a person from running. A loud sickening scream filled the air as Juan absorbed spray. He was impaled on the spiked fence he had tried to jump over.

Jim immediately went downstairs and into the yard. He lifted the lifeless body of Juan from the spikes.

As Jim went back into the house, he noticed George's son, Albert, hiding in the kitchen, and wondered how he could be involved in the tragedy.

George, who had been in the bar a block away, drinking, approached the house out of curiosity, and when he entered the room he saw Jim putting handcuffs on Albert.

"Hey," George shouted. "What are you doing to my boy? You've got to leave him alone, Jim. I'll do anything to make it up. Are you all right Albert?"

Albert looked around a little dazed. He didn't see Juan so thought he had gotten away. He knew of the threat on his life and he was afraid to say anything. Albert nodded his head slowly.

George noticed the shoe in the plastic bag which was on the floor. He stooped over and picked it up and at the same time pulled Jim's gun from his holster.

"Come on now, George. You're drunk, so give me the bag and the gun. You're making things worse. You're digging a hole for yourself, that's all," Jim remonstrated.

George wanted to get rid of the shoe because he thought his son had taken part in the henious act.

"Jim," George was pointing the gun at Jim. "You can't go through with this. The racial thing is bad enough, but with the . . . the shoe business on top . . . if you take in my son he'll never see daylight again."

Albert realized he should say something, but all he got out was, "Dad!"

For a brief moment George had a vision of his childhood days. He was seated at a piano and the music stared in front of him. The child had a mental block between his head and his fingers. He never got past the first line of *Poor Butterfly*. George, the man, thought he had no mental block now between his fingers and the trigger. The shot was fired at Jim's chest. He let his hands drop to his sides and he looked at Jim who had a shocked, suprised stare in his eyes.

Jim quietly took the bag and the gun from George. "I guess you know you could have killed me, but the bullet-proof vest saved me." Jim quickly put some cuffs on George. A patrolman came in to help Jim.

As the officer held George, Albert spoke up. "Dad, you should have asked me for a story before you did any shooting. I didn't think you would take the gun and fire it. I had nothing to do with the rape, in fact, I tried to stop Juan from molesting the lady with the shoe."

The alcohol was slowly leaving his system and George realized what a big mistake he had made. The booze had ruined him, but he had been unable to leave it alone since his wife died. Coming out of his stupor, George said, "Son, what were you doing here?"

"I was supposed to pick up some grass from Juan, but I didn't know the guy would get crazy," Albert answered.

"So you're on that stuff. Well, don't ever go to heroin. Look at me . . . at the mess . . . because I'm always drunk. I guess I'll die in jail." George's head pointed to the floor. Suddenly his head moved upward and he asked, "Son, why didn't you speak up sooner?"

"I was afraid of Juan. He told me if I ever said anything about his dope selling he would kill me."

Jim heard the last part of Albert's answer and said, "Juan won't be killing anybody. He's gone to the morgue. I used the spray on him, because he wanted to jump and clear the spikes on the fence. The spray stopped him from completing the jump and he fell on the spikes," Jim explained.

"I know it's asking for too much, Jim, but ain't there something you can do?" George begged.

"Nothing, George. You took that shot at me. Remember what you told me. You said I should make lots of pinches, so how can I leave this one go? It would kill my career. Sorry."

"I was a drunken fool, Jim . . . I was wrong . . . dead wrong!" repeated George.

"You worked up a mess, George. Just hope that your son will pull out of it."

"Maybe you can go easy on him, Jim," George pleaded.

"Well, you know it's not up to me, George, but I'm sure the judge will be fair. Albert will probably get by with a few years of probation."

The police car was ready to take George and Albert to the station. An ambulance picked up Juan's body.

Carlos was on his way home from the pool room when he found Adolph barely conscious. He rolled up Adolph's trousers to find a steady flow of blood. Taking off his white shirt, he wrapped it around the leg below the wound and away from the heart. This would stop the blood flow from a vein.

"You'll be all right, Adolph. I'll go and call an ambulance," Carlos assured.

Adolph labored to speak, asking, "What happened to Jeanne?"

Carlos couldn't wait to hear the story. When he returned, the ambulance had arrived. Adolph was rushed to the hospital where a doctor said that the tourniquet had saved his life.

Later in the day Don got a call from Carlos who was disturbed when he heard of the horrible crime. He felt guilty for telling Juan about the letter that Jeanne had written.

"I called the hospital, Carlos. Adolph and his niece are getting along fine." Don spoke quietly.

"I still can't feel well over this thing," Carlos lamented.

"What's bothering you, Carlos?"

"I'd rather not discuss it over the phone."

"All right, I'll stop in and we'll talk it over before I go to work," Don said.

A few simple furnishings greeted Don as he entered Carlos' room.

"You seem to look anything but contented, Carlos."

"Well, Don, I sometimes go to the pool room on Saturday mornings, but I couldn't today because that's the place I was coming from when I found poor Adolph. I'm glad to hear that he and his niece are doing fine, but I have to tell you about the letter."

"What letter?" questioned Don.

"It was a letter that Adolph got from his niece, a sort of . . . love letter," Carlos revealed.

Don tilted his head backwards. "Oh, that," he said. "How did you know?"

"That's what's been bothering me. I looked at the letter during one of my crazy moods, then in a crazier mood I told Juan about the letter. I had no idea he was a dope pusher and a guy who would rape." Carlos supported his chin with his hand.

"Well, I wasn't supposed to know about the letter, but when Adolph showed it to Joe Clark, Joe then passed the news to me with the admonition to keep it to myself. The tragedy could not have been foreseen, Carlos. You saved Adolph's life by applying the tourniquet." Don thought for a moment then said, "I know you won't be working tomorrow so maybe we can get together at William's restaurant. I would like you to meet a friend of mine, Bill Burk. He's the top clerk on our shift."

"That'll be fine with me," Carlos answered.

"Be there at two-forty-five."

"I'll be there," Carlos promised.

At two-forty-five, Don, Carlos and Bill Burk were ordering a junior meal at Williams.

"I'm pleased to meet a friend of Don's," Bill Burk said, extending his hand.

"Same here," said Carlos.

As Bill took a bite of the sandwich he reflected that if he would testify in the State Crimes Commission's hearings, he would be useless in gaining further evidence against the dope ring.

"I understand that Jim is on the narcotics squad, Don. I just thought of something. Carlos, how would you like to be helping the Crime Commission? I'm going to testify against the dope outfit. I've decided to go straight. I'm tired of seeing kids getting into trouble, and dying from overdose."

Don smiled for he was going to suggest the same idea that Bill Burk was talking about.

"Sounds exciting," said Carlos. "I think I'd like to."

"Well, right after I see Jim, I'll introduce you to the man who will introduce you to the pusher. His name is Steve Thomas. Jim will be glad to have your help." Bill poured more coffee into his system. "He'll remind you to turn any purchases over to him." Bill plunked down the tip. "He wouldn't like you to become a junkie."

Later, Steve Thomas drove Carlos over to the Ben Franklin School. Shaky Dave was sitting on a bench, beating out a slow beat, signifying there was stuff available for the regular customers. Shaky was bearded and wore a wide-brim Stetson, and was fitted with army boots.

"I'm Steve Thomas," Steve said as he advanced to the bench.

Shaky looked at a little book he tried to hide in the back of his drum.

"Right. You're okay, Steve," Shaky said. He added, "I'm Dave. They call me Shaky Dave." Shaky shook a little to demonstrate.

"I want to introduce a good friend of mine. Meet Carlos — Carlos Gonzales."

"All right, Carlos. I got to put you down in the book."

"Is it okay to go to the house now?" asked Steve.

"We got a new one now. It's at 1605 Buttonwood. Are you going now?"

"Yes. We would like to," Steve added.

"Give me a chance to go over and open up the place. You're the first to go in the new place," said Shaky.

"Okay, we'll stop and have one before going there."

"Watch out for the fuzz," Shaky admonished.

Twenty minutes later, Steven and Carlos picked their fix and the sale was completed.

CHAPTER 7

Carlos and Don had just returned from a visit to the hospital where Adolph and his niece, Jeanne, were doing much better. They were chatting in Don's apartment.

"How do you like helping in the narcotic investigation, Carlos?"

"It's all right, but I'm still bugged with that stupid act of mine that caused so much trouble for everyone. I think trouble is too mild a word to describe it, however." Carlos hung his head.

"Do you have a girl friend?" Don asked.

"No. Do you think I'd do better if I had one?"

"Of course. If you have the right one. I can introduce you to Alice. She was at the Society Hall too, and she's lovely. She majored in art, and I'm sure your drawings will appeal to her.

Don obtained Alice's phone number from Albert, and she agreed to meet Carlos in the Dallas home.

She was well co-ordinated, her walk was an easy glide and Carlos fell in love with her. She was super.

She knew Carlos had great talent, and thought he was a great guy. She was ready to introduce him to her parents.

On Tuesday night around six when Don went to William's to eat, he noticed a man looking at the cars parked in front of the store. His, the manager's and Bill Burk's were among them. Don had never seen the gent before, and at the moment didn't think much about it. The man was white, around forty or so and built on the husky side. He wore a special shoe for one leg was shorter.

It was when the men were ready to go home that night that Don noticed the hood of Bill's car slightly open. Bill was already seated at the wheel but the door was open.

Don ran over and grabbed Bill's arm and pulled him out of the car and toward the front entrance of the store. They laid there on the store step hugging the door as the bomb went off. Glass and debris fell all around when the car blew up.

The only mishap to their bodies was a scratch that Bill got when he put his hand on a piece of glass getting up from the step.

"It looks like somebody doesn't care too much about the idea that I'm appearing at the Crimes Commission hearings," Bill stated after he regained his breath.

"I saw a creep hanging around here when I went to lunch. I could kick myself for not calling the police then," said Don.

Jim and his partner arrived shortly, and Don described the man.

"It looks like a contract job. The man you saw was probably the hit man, Don," Jim advised.

Jim took Don downtown to look at some mug shots, but he was unable to identify any of the pictures as the man he saw.

Bill Burk had his car towed to the junk yard the next day after the crime lab had taken photographs and fingerprints. He was grateful that he was still around, even if he did have to buy a new car.

Don later asked Bill, "Who tried to kill you?"

"It must have been that phony Jack Slaton. Who else? He'll be surprised and disgusted when he learns I'm still alive."

"A state trooper was assigned to protect the home of Bill Burk, until the trials were over.

The day's work finished, Jim was driving home for a hot meal with his wife, Mable, and son, Kevin. It was strange that he should be thinking of how to get more evidence on the dope ring, and at the same time he was going over some of the lines in the book the fellows at the store had given him — *Success, the Magnetic Method.* It started to rain, dimming the view of the tugboat emitting its warning sound. It was nudging the *Cypress* which would unload a cargo from Turkey in the morning.

As he approached Pier 39 North, he saw a girl, her jacket lying on the ground beside her, about to take a dive. Jim opened his car door and pounced on the girl, leading her away from the wharf.

"Come and sit in my car and get out of the rain," Jim spoke kindly to her.

She was around twenty, a blonde with small features. She wore a red mini dress with a showy neckline, and had on black pantyhose. Jim threw the wet gray jacket to the rear of the car and wrapped his own around her shoulders.

His reasoning told him that the girl normally could radiate a picture of health, but her appearance now suggested the use of drugs.

He thought of the magnetic method, knowing he would have an elevating influence on her if he used the right way, but how could he work it?

"I'm Jim Smith of the narcotic squad," Jim began, his face lighting up with a gentleness as he showed the girl his badge.

"Of all the guys driving on this road it would have to be a detective," she lamented.

"You don't have to be so upset about meeting a detective. What's so horrible about me?" Jim asked.

"It's not you I'm thinking about. It's my father, Walter Willard," the girl whined.

"You're the commissioner's daughter?" Jim's mouth didn't close for a moment.

"Now you know what's so horrible. Please . . . I'm his daughter, Sylvia, and please . . . isn't there some way that my father won't hear about this?" Her eyes searched Jim's.

Jim thought magnetically and otherwise. "I'll tell you what. I'm supposed to take you to the Hospital and get a report, but because I'm heading home, would you like to come along? You can be spared the clinical aspect."

"Anything but that hospital routine," she whimpered.

Jim and Sylvia left the car and entered his apartment, which was unmatched with her father's suite at 2600 Parkway. Sylvia brightened up as soon as she met Jim's wife, Mabel and son Kevin.

Forgetting the magnetic approach, Jim asked, "Sylvia, what made you go down to the wharf?"

After Kevin left the room to watch TV, Sylvia grabbed a cigarette from her purse and said, "I might as well tell you. Maybe I'll go straight.

Pardon me for smoking, but I'm still bunched up.

"My boy friend was Jack Slaton until I found out the creep was cheating on me. I saw him going into a hotel with a woman. He owns the Delaware Cafe and he's also a top man in the dope racket. That's why I can't let my dad find out. You won't tell him, will you?"

"I won't tell about your boy friend," Jim agreed.

"Oh yeah, the wharf business." Sylvia pulled the cigarette from her lips. "The wharf thing — I must have gone on a bummer. Don't worry. There's no pot in this cigarette, but I had some grass earlier and I guess it put me on a bummer trip. I went bananas, but I beg you not to let my father know," Sylvia implored.

"All right, Sylvia, but I'll have to insist you allow me to call your home to have someone pick you up. I can say you didn't feel well."

Jim made the call and in ten minutes a motorcycle escorted car arrived to take Sylvia home.

At nine o'clock, Jim called the Willard home and was finally able to talk with Mr. Willard himself. "Commissioner, I hope you forgive me, but I thought you could make the decision better," Jim said.

"What decision? Who are you?" the commissioner snapped.

Jim introduced himself, then told Willard of his daughter's attempted suicide.

"She really wanted to jump?" Willard's tone was more friendly.

"That's the way it looked, Commissioner," Jim recounted.

"Thanks for calling, Mr. Smith. Good night."

Jim met with Carlos Gonzales periodically at Second and Market Streets to get any dope purchases that Carlos was able to make. This evening he had only one pack to give Jim, then he said, "Shaky is playing the fast beat on the bongo drum again."

"Thanks Carlos. See you later." Jim got into his car and wheeled it down to the Delaware Cafe. He didn't have to wait long before Slaton came out and got into his Cadillac. Jim took a chance and followed the Caddy, and sure enough, the Caddy rolled down Broad Street, slowed down at the Ben Franklin school where the driver waved at Shaky. The Caddy then picked up speed, but the traffic was such that Jim was able to keep up.

Slaton stopped in the shadow of the big bulkhead of the Cypress and used a pay phone.

Jim, parked on the other side of the avenue, saw a man hand Slaton a package, then Slaton got into his Caddy and sped along Deleware Avenue to where the green and purple neon lights beckoned the patrons. The Caddy pulled in to the parking lot and Jim pulled in behind him.

A waiter bowed as Jack walked in, saying, "Good evening Mr. Slaton."

So he's Slaton, the guy Violet had called a prostitute in Tom's Cafe, the night she tried to rob George Dallas, Jim thought. He took a good look at Slaton. He was twenty-five, wore a high pompadour and had a dimpled chin. He was wearing bell-bottom trousers, white buck shoes and there was a silver key chain hanging from his belt.

He walked, carrying the package, to the rear of the room and ascended the stairs.

Jim sat down at the table and ordered a steak sandwich with gravy. The gravy always improved his appetite because of its unique aroma. He also ordered a coke. He was thinking of obtaining a search and seizure warrant and of a subsequent raid when Sylvia came in.

She walked up to Jim, and said, "Oh, that sandwich smells good."

"Sit down for a minute, Sylvia. Would you like a sandwich?"

"No thanks. I just had something to eat, but I would like a ginger ale."

"What brings you down here?" Jim questioned.

"Jack and I made up."

"Made up? What do you mean, Sylvia?"

"Well, he called me and told me the woman I saw him with was meeting him just for a business deal. She had an office in the hotel," explained Sylvia, pulling her shoulder down a bit. "I might even go for a fix."

"Sylvia, don't be a fool! Jack Slaton worked as a prostitute in New York!"

"I don't think I should believe that," Sylvia retorted.

The head waiter gingerly approached the area where Jim and Sylvia sat.

"I'll prove it to you," Jim announced.

They walked over to the phone that was on the southern wall next to the men's room. The acoustics were such that in one of the toilet booths a listener could hear someone on the phone. Phillip, the head waiter went to that booth and listened.

"Hello, Stanley." Jim was speaking to the bartender at Tom's Cafe. "Listen, you know the guy who wanted you to throw out Violet, the girl who took George Dallas' wallet?"

"Well, do me a favor and tell this young lady what Violet called Jack Slaton that night," Jim slipped the phone to Sylvia.

"What did she call him, Stanley?" Sylvia asked.

"Oh no! Are you sure she said a prostitute?

"It's a strange piece of news to thank you for, but you have been helpful. Thanks." Sylvia hung up quickly.

As they walked back to the table, they saw the head waiter emerge from the men's room and hurry upstairs to tell his boss what he had heard.

The Delaware Tavern was not the only place where the conversation was overheard. Next door to the tavern, in a rooming house, Carlos Gonzales was listening to a small receiver. The sound from the receiver was fed into a tape recorder. Carlos listened carefully to the speech Slaton was making in the office next door.

"Guys, we have to do something about Miller. He buggered up the job on Bill Burk, and I don't need a lousy hit man like him."

Jack Slaton was resounding with such anger as to make Carlos call Don at his apartment.

"Don, I got it all on tape for you. Are you coming over?"

"I'll be right there, Carlos. Keep the tape rolling."

Don pulled up with his Galaxie in front of the rooming house.

"We might as well listen to the cassette," Carlos said, turning on the playback.

After Jack Slaton told about being angry with his hit man, the head waiter came into the office and approached Slaton. Jack turned in his swivel chair to listen to Phillip, the waiter. The tape then revealed the rest of the conversation.

"There's a man sitting at a table over near the south wall with a girl named Sylvia. He called some place and talked to a man named Stanley. He then handed the phone to Sylvia. Boss, Stanley told Sylvia that some female called you a prostitute." Phillip shook his head in disbelief.

Jack Slaton opened the door and took a few steps down the stairway, then quickly returned to his desk and addressed the waiter. "Thanks, Phillip," the reocrder at the rooming house played. I'll see you later." The voice was really low with "That's Sylvia all right." Then as the voice got louder, it continued, "Oh, that's the game. I'll change my plans and have that lousy hit man go after Sylvia, then we'll take care of him too."

Carlos removed the cassette to put in a fresh one. The recorder held two cartridges.

"Carlos, we're getting somewhere. The idea of the tapes was suggested by Hal Kenny, our State Attorney General. At the beginning of the probe we placed an ad in all papers in the state, promising lucrative rewards for any information pertaining to the illegal use or sale of drugs, with all disclosures held confidential. Jay Fontain, one of Slaton's henchmen answered the ad. He hid the tiny transmitter in Slaton's office, and that's what we're listening to, Carlos."

"Isn't this henchman taking a big risk?" questions Don's helper.

"Definitely, but he's getting handsome checks from the state sent to a post office box, and he hates Slaton's guts. He thinks Slaton is paying his henchman with crumbs. Have you got enough cassettes?"

"I have six. That should be plenty for a while," Carlos answered.

"I'm going next door, Carlos, and you're doing a good job. Just as you did with the illustrations. Thanks. How's Alice?"

"Fine, Don."

"You didn't propose yet?" asked Don.

"Later," Carlos perked up.

Don stood for a moment inside the cafe. At a table in the center, he recognized the man he had seen around Bill's car the night of the explosion. Don sat at a spot a few tables away from the hit man. As he reflected on how he could apply the magnetic theory, Bob Miller got up to put a coin in the juke box. Don noticed the special shoe he wore. With his memory refreshed, he remembered that Max Miller had told him about a nephew who had one leg shorter than the other.

Jim, who was sitting with Sylvia, looked up and saw Don.

The music diffused, "Poor Butterfly, and as she smiles through her tears."

"What brings you down here, Don?" Jim asked.

"I'll explain later, Jim." Don showed Jim a card which read, 'I'm with you.' Don smiled and simply said, "See you."

The song went on, "She murmurs low," as Jim took his seat alongside Sylvia.

Slaton came out of his office and leaned over the railing, asking the waiter to tell Miller to come into the office. Don overheard the waiter saying, "Mr. Miller, you're wanted in the office."

When Miller finally returned to his table, the music continued, "Then I never sigh or cry — Poor butterfly."

Don moved to Miller's table, remarking, "Excuse me for being so bold, but I heard the waiter calling your name. I know a Max Miller who told me he had a nephew with one leg shorter than the other. I was curious."

"I have an uncle named Max. What do you know about him?" Miller asked.

"I gave him some exercises which helped him greatly. He walks without a cane now."

"That's mighty nice of you, but I can tell you one thing. Uncle Max never had to struggle like me. I got five kids to support — all boys and if you pardon the expression," Miller stopped to down some beer. "The one who is thirteen, I'll swear his thing is always hard."

Don thought it was time to tell Miller. He pointed to the table where Sylvia was and said, "See that girl with the red dress? She's the Police Commissioner's daughter."

"Commissioner's daughter!" Miller took a fast gulp of the hops and malt. "Are you sure?"

"Yes. I'm not only sure of it, but I also know they're not going to let you live whether you complete the job or not, Mr. Miller."

"How do you know that?" There was a slight tremble in Miller's hand as he brought down the glass.

"Let me say it this way. You're supposed to get rid of the girl, aren't you?"

Miller sensed the significance of the question, and said, "You're the law, huh?"

Don put down his wine glass and smiled. "I'll say part of it, Mr. Miller."

Miller opened and closed his hands alternately. "I guess I asked for it."

Don noting that Miller was all whipped up, said, "Five sons. You know Mr. Miller, you wouldn't want any of your sons to become junkies. What chance have you got to get away with the murder of the commissioner's daughter. You'll be hounded by every man of the law that they can spare."

The waves of music continued with *Poor Butterfly* as Don enjoyed the light moselle wine.

Bob Miller put his head straight back in the chair and looked at the ceiling. "I wonder who the 'Poor Butterfly' is," he said. He rose quickly after another intake of beer. "I got to check something out."

Don's eyes followed the large frame as he headed for the stairway.

The office door opened, closed, then opened again. Slaton and Miller came down the staircase.

"Before we talk, let's have a drink," Miller suggested.

Slaton ordered a scotch and Miller a beer.

Miller waited long enough for Slaton to knock off his shot of liquor then screwed up his face and said in anger, "You told me to be sure and not slip up on the job, but you didn't tell me she's the commissioner's daughter. You'd better tell me now . . . or I'll go over and ask her."

Slaton looked at the table where Don sat and answered, "Yeah. What have you been doing? Sitting with the law? You're pretty tricky taking me away from my men. It won't help you," said Slaton, moving his hand in the direction of his gun. Miller went for his thirty-eight special, but lost in the element of time.

The shot rang out just as the song reached, "I just mus' die, poor Butterfly."

Don had been watching the men, and he reached for something in his pocket but he knew it was no use. Miller had already dropped to the floor and his blood was spilling. Slaton ran to his office.

The music played on, "But if he don't come back." The tears were rolling down Miller's cheeks as his eyes met Don's. "Tell my wife I'm sorry I couldn't make it to . . . care," Miller talked with great effort. He tried to squeeze Don's hand, and Don could just about apprehend his last words, "Five boys . . . no . . . junkies."

Slaton directed his gunmen to remove Miller's body to a station wagon at the rear of the tavern. He was so absorbed in the job of moving the body that he forgot to lock the front door.

Don, in the meantime, used a small transmitter and called Carlos next door, asking him to bring in two guns. The guns were in a desk drawer and Carlos then hurried back to the rooming house to take care of his pick up units.

Slaton waved to the gunmen as they marched down the aisle. "Come on guys. We've got work here." Pointing to one of the men, Slaton ordered him to search Jim. Jim's gun was taken and so was his badge.

At Slaton's request, another henchman took hold of Sylvia. Slaton looked toward the center table and saw Don. "Get that creep," he shouted. "He's the guy who was talking to Miller."

As the gunman moved toward him, Don fired his pistol up at the ceiling, then edged closer to the men holding Sylvia removing an object from his coat pocket. He sprayed the gas over the racketeers.

All of their guns dropped immediately to the floor, and Slaton was the first to cry out, "I don't have any feeling in my fingers! Hey, what the hell's going on?"

The other guys had the same complaint. "Boss, I can't use my fingers," they complained.

Slaton shouted for the bartender to come over. "Hey, Tony. We'll kick our guns over to you and you can pick them up."

Tony picked up the guns and hid all but one under the bar, then he aimed his weapon at Don. Don gave one big squirt from his spray gun and Tony's fingers went numb.

Don used his transmitter again and asked Carlos to call.

By this time Jim realized that Don was involved in the enforcement of the law and was not just playing a Good Samaritan role.

After the gang was taken into custody Don shook hands with Jim saying, "I guess you know I'm working for the state. I'm sorry I had to keep things so secretive, but you do understand, Jim?"

"Yes, I understand. Let me introduce you to the Commissioner's daughter, Sylvia Willard," Jim said.

"Pleased to know you," Don said, shaking her hand.

"I must take her home or her father might demote me," said Jim, then quickly added, "What was that stuff you were spraying around?"

"Well, Jim. You were the one who gave me the idea. Remember about a year and a half ago you told us about the spray that would temporarily stop a person from running. Well, that gave me the idea of having a spray made that would stop one from using the fingers. The effect would also be a temporary paralysis. That gang will be able to use their fingers again in a half hour."

"I must say it's wonderful. It kept them from shooting," Jim answered.

The last of the Miller's coins were now used up and the music trailed off with "I just mus' die, Poor Butterfly."

"Maybe I can see you after I take Sylvia home," Jim inquired.

"I think it would be better if we meet in William's in the morning, Jim."

"Okay. That'll give me a chance to pick up Shaky Dave, the dope pusher."

"Right, Jim. Good night. Good night, Sylvia. I'm sorry I can't take more time to talk with you."

The two met for an early morning breakfast. "It's unusual for you to have breakfast here," said Jim after they were seated.

"Yes. My job at the liquor store is over. You know — the nature of the work. I'm too well-known in the city now, so I'll most likely be asked to work in another town," Don answered.

"Your undercover work has helped me. The boss promoted me. I should say I've been promoted to Sergeant and it appears as though I'll make lieutenant soon," Jim said with excitement.

A blonde waitress came up and took their orders. "Some eggs, scrambled and toast, potatoes and coffee, please." Jim ordered.

"I'll have scrambled eggs, toast and orange juice," ordered Don.

"I'll be missing you and the fellows, Jim, but of course you will always be welcome at the Society Hall. My father will be presiding again, and you'll be pleased with his presentations, I'm sure."

The waitress was prompt with their orders.

Jim listened to Don's explanation. "We did it in a different way than the F.B.I. I was placed in the liquor store before they transferred Bill Burk there, and I was able to save his life so it turned out all right. We could have," Don tasted the orange juice, "we could have planted a man in the store where Bill worked, but it was agreed that I should gain the experience first."

Jim ate some of the toast. "I think that was a great idea," he said.

"Yes, but I hate to think about having to testify against my friend, George, when his case is before the court," Jim added. "The poor guy lost his head when his wife died."

Their breakfast specials were now eaten, and Don paid for the check, and they left William's lunch place.

After the final rites for Bob Miller, Don surprised Max Miller and his sister, Edna with a meal after they attended the early synagogue services.

"Are you leaving town?" Max asked as they were waiting for their order.

"Yes, my new job. I'll keep in touch with you."

The meal was brought, and for each there was a good portion of fresh smaltz herring, a large boiled potato, a big slice of onion, rye bread and a glass of tea.

"I wouldn't ask for anything more," said Max, enjoying the food.

"We thank you very much," said Edna. "We'll always remember how good you've been to us.

"And, I'll always think of you," Don said. He then saw them safely to their home.

CHAPTER 8

Albert's trial was held on a Monday two months later. There was no jury, as Jim spoke to the judge on the advisability of a suspended sentence. Albert had been taking courses in medicine and Jim thought it would be wise if he could continue. Consequently, Albert was placed on three years probation.

A jury was present, however, at George's trial a month later. Jim would have preferred not to testify, but it was necessary. The jury brought in a guilty verdict, and the judge sentenced him to seven years in jail.

"I can't ignore the fact that you could have killed a police officer," the judge advised.

Before Don went away he gave Carlos a complete set of books on the magnetic theory, and Carlos lost no time in mastering the art. Carlos promised Don that he would lend a hand to Albert when needed.

Albert and Carlos rode up to Somerdale Prison every weekend to see George. George had been in there a year when Albert told him he was taking piano lessons and learning to play *Poor Butterfly*.

This brought memories of his own childhood when he never was able to get past the first half of the third line, "The moments pass into hours."

"Son, that's great. You made out where I failed. How is college going?"

"Good, Dad. In four years I should be hanging out my shingle."

"Four years," George sighed. "The lawyer was here today and said he was unable to get the sentence lowered. I won't even be out in five."

"Don't be too discouraged, Dad. I saw Jim on Tuesday. You know he's sergeant now," Albert said.

George turned his head away.

"It's not the way you think, Dad. Jim said the reason he hasn't come to see you is that he wouldn't be of any help."

"That's all right, son. I understand. The next time you see him, tell him I feel miserable everytime I think of the awful thing I did," George lamented with a twitching chin.

Visiting time was over and the farewells were always tough.

"I'll see you next week."

Flora continued teaching piano to Albert, and on this evening late in May after Albert was through studying, he played *Poor Butterfly* on the piano while Flora made a tape recording of it. When the recording was finished, Albert gazed at the lips he loved to kiss.

"Albert, you're in deep thought," Flora said as she caught the mien.

"Yes," Albert confessed. "In less than two years my probation ends, and it should be a good time to propose."

"I can wait, Albert. I'm not thinking of changing boy friends." Flora laughed.

"It will also be closer to the time for me to hang out my shingle," Albert rejoined, then prepared to take Flora home.

On Father's Day, Albert and Flora rode out to Somerdale Prison. "A gift for my dad," said Albert joyfully, handing the package to the guard.

"Dad, it's a tape recording of *Poor Butterfly* that I played for you," explained Albert. "I hope they'll let you play it. It's a battery operated recorder, so if you need batteries let me know."

"It was very thoughtful of you, son. Thanks. I guess the fancy name for what I'm going through is called an emotional crisis. The song might be of some help."

After Flora and Albert said good-bye, George played the tape for the guard. They listened to the tune, "Neath the blossoms waiting," and when there was silence, George asked, "What do you think?"

The guard thought it over, then said, "Why not. Just don't play it too loud." He gave George a wink.

"You're good people, guard. Thanks a lot." George extended his hand and the guard understood as he led George back to the cell.

The trial of Jack Slaton was held July 8th. Sylvia, Bill Burk, Jim Smith and Don Ellsman were witnesses for the prosecution.

The trial lasted three days and the jury returned a guilty verdict. The judge sentenced Slaton to ninety-nine years.

Time passed quickly and Albert was no longer on the probation list. He announced this to his father with the news, "Dad, I'm getting married next month," he said.

"I'm sorry I can't be at the wedding, son. So Flora will be a June bride. How nice," George responded.

"Yes, Dad. She'll be one of the brides. Alice and Carlos will be the other half of our double wedding."

"Carlos?" George was not too sure.

"Yes. He's the fellow who rooms at Adolph's house."

"Oh yeah. I recall now. He's the guy who draws a lot," remembered George.

"We're getting married in the little church on the corner. Does that sound familiar?"

"Indeed it does. It was there I married your mother. Good bless her," George said sadly.

"I'm sorry, Dad, you won't be there. Flora could not come today for she has a bad cold. Jim gave me the new address of Don, so we sent them an invitation."

"Good, son. Tell Flora to take care of her health. I don't have a present, but . . . " George closed his eyes briefly then continued, "I'm not the right guy to be giving anybody advice, so I hope everything turns out all right. Tell the other couple — oh yeah, Alice and Carlos — I wish them the best of everything."

"I'll do that. Look at it this way, Dad," Albert tried to look cheerful. "You're at the halfway mark." Albert's voice choked.

"Yeah, son. Maybe the next half will be easier," George smiled.

"I'll see you after the wedding, dad."

"Better say after the honeymoon," George winked.

Four more years of confinement slowly passed. All the time George wondered why he took the gun out of Jim's holster and fired point blank at him.

He was thinking of his stupid act when Albert arrived, but he was not alone. George was surprised to see Jim.

"Here's a stranger, Dad."

"I'm really glad to see you, Jim," George said.

"Me too," answered Jim. "I haven't been bitter. I just waited until I could root for your parole. I'm Captain now, and maybe my rooting will help."

A smile crossed George's face. "I hope I live long enough to do something good for you, Jim." George offered his hand.

"Another thing, George. I was speaking to Adolph, and he's about to retire. If you would like to take his job I can talk to the manager."

"Why not? I'll have to pay bills, and I doubt whether I could get a better job."

"Okay, George. I'll tell the manager to keep you in mind."

Before leaving the prison, Albert spoke up. "I'm waiting for you to come home before I hang out my shingle, Dad."

There was a tear in George's eye as Albert took his leave.

George obtained his freedom just a week later. There were flowers on the table and champagne ready on ice at the Dallas home. Don, also flew in from Pittsburgh to attend.

"I'm very grateful for all you've done, Don," George said.

"That's what friendship is all about, George. Jim told me you can take over Adolph's old job as soon as you are ready."

"I hope the winos don't make fun about my being in jail," George worried.

"Jim told me he talked to Joe Clark at the store, and Joe is going to tell Freddy the Fisherman, Jake the Fake and Charlie the Joker to be considerate, so I don't think you'll be bothered much," said Don. "I'm heading back to Pittsburgh, George. God bless you. I'll keep in touch."

"Bless you and tell the wife and kid I wish them well."

After the homecoming was over, George sat in a chair in the front room that would become the office of Dr. Albert Dallas. George would have a room in the back.

Albert had already told his father about the break he was getting from the police department through Jim's efforts, and he would be assisting in working for the improvement of the spray that disabled a person from running. A fund had been established to insure the use of the spray without side effects.

George relaxed and was listening to a black comedian on the TV.

"We black people are not afraid anymore. We stopped being afraid after getting pushed around for four hundred years," said the comedian.

The comedian didn't say the blacks were no longer afraid of just white people.

All that time in prison George had not understood why he took a shot at his friend, Jim, in that vacant house on Spring Street.

58

It came like a jolt as George thought the comedian pinpointed the reason, or to be more accurate, the cause. George thought the constant reminder not to be afraid had pervaded his brain. At the time, George had convinced himself that he had no fear of Jim, an officer of the law.

Then George thought *"how punchy can anybody get?"* He thought he just had to be afraid of something, but why should he walk in front of a truck coming down the street?

George took over Adolph's job the next week, and his old friends were very kind.

That same day, Albert started his practice. Although his patients were not many, he kept busy because of the research work he was engaged in at the police lab.

Don finished his book titled, *Applied Magnetic Secrets,* and sent a copy to each of his friends. In the foreword, he had much praise for the illustrations done by Carlos.

In five years, Albert's practice increased so much that he could no longer handle the research work at the police lab. He moved his office to the center of town, and also leased an apartment on the Parkway.

On Mother's Day of that year, Dr. Dallas, Alice and their son, Albert, Jr., who was now nearly four years old, were at George's. Albert had just finished playing *Poor Butterfly* on the old piano.

George looked tired when he picked up his grandson, but he gave the child a friendly pat on the head and handed him a small toy before putting him down.

"Albert," said George. "I'd like to drive to the cemetery alone. You can stop over there later. All right, son?"

"Sure, Dad. We'll see you then."

George took the tape recorder to the grave site. He looked at the stone with his wife's name, Mary Dallas, and said the prayer of mourning. He got up from the kneeling position and turned on the set to a low volume.

As the sound of the music floated along the graves, George dreamed. It could not be the same dream of years ago — a dream that he would become a big guy in police work, or even a dream that he was a manager of a liquor store. It could be nothing else but to push a broom.

He dreamed of the night when Nick Gross brought that girl, Violet, to his table at the tavern. It was truly the only time he had the idea in his head about a woman. She then stole his wallet.

Suddenly, George stopped dreaming in time to hear the line of the song. The music was soft, familiar and the words 'The moon and I know that he be faithful, I'm sure he'll come to be by and by.'

George peacefully closed his eyes and rested his head upon the grave.

CHAPTER 9

While Adolph was still working at the liquor store, he met Sadie Soler in the supermarket from time to time. She was a thin woman of medium height, and she loved to wear brightly colored clothes. She was in her late seventies.

Sadie's husband, Herman Solder, M.D., had died two years earlier. Sadie had worked for him as his nurse and they lived over the doctor's office at the northwest corner of Tenth and Pearl Streets. She had a girl when she was thirty, but didn't have a boy until fourteen years later. She called her son Herman, Jr., a chemical baby because her husband had taken all kinds of medicine to impregnate her.

Herman, Jr. attended a college to learn electrical engineering, but dropped out after one year. He then joined the Signal Corps, and after three years of service, he married Josephine.

After their four children arrived, Herman decided to build a house in Jersey. He helped in the woodwork and became so interested that carpentry became his occupation, but because he drank a lot and was unable to pay the bills, they lost the house and their marriage was over. Josephine moved and took the kids with her to her mother's house in Willow Grove. Herman went back to Philly to live with his parents.

After Herman's father died, Sadie worried about her son not getting sex, so she took him to parties where there were both blacks and whites present. One party they attended, everything was going all right until some dude tried to steal Sadie's handbag. She screamed and scared the crook away, then she grabbed Herman by the hand and left. They didn't attend those kind of parties any more. Sadie, however, died the following year, and not long after Herman fell ill with epilepsy.

He worked as a carpenter for a contractor on Broad Street, and when he got paid he looked for a girl. It was difficult to find a white girl, so Herman picked up Marie, a young black girl. She was short and husky and wore her hair long. She made many visits to Herman's house until Herman lost his job, then Marie's visits were fewer.

Toward the end of 1959, Herman got a break and met a widow in a taproom. She was white, fifteen years older than Herman, but willing to shell out and pay some bills just for some loving.

She stayed with Herman for about a year, but in 1961 Rosie told him she was going to California to get a job, but Herman figured she was going after another guy.

Adolph was still trying to improve his sexual skill in April of 1961, and he inadvertently met Herman in Bill's taproom. He told Herman about his chats with his mother. Herman remembered his mother talking about Adolph. While the two were talking, Herman was eyeing a black girl.

"You like the black ones?" Adolph asked.

"There aren't many white ones around here anymore." Herman put the beer down for a moment and leaned towards Adolph. "I'll tell you one thing though. I think the black ones carry the best asses around with them." He paused for a drink, then went on. "They really got 'em. Take that Marie who comes around to see me. I like the looks of her ass."

"Does she charge?" Adolph asked, relinquishing his hold on the beer glass.

"Charge?" Herman appeared to be studying his drinking partner. "Oh, when I get a job I give her some bucks. If she's hot, I can knock off a hunk for almost nothing. I remember one time I only had a quarter to give her . . . ."

Herman was killing his thirst much faster than Adolph. He had had two more glasses in quick order. "Do you know what Marie likes to do?" he asked.

Adolph put his glass down slowly. "What's that?" he questioned.

"She'll get undressed and tell me to chase her all over the house," explained Herman in a grogging style.

"Doesn't that make you tired before you can do anything?" Adolph was curious.

Herman gave Adolph that long, drunken look, came down on the bar with the glass again and said loudly, "That's when I taste it."

"Taste it?" Adolph seemed puzzled.

"Yeah, I kissed that black meat, and you want to know something? My father left a ton of medical books in those bookcases back in my shack and nowhere does it say that anybody died from it." Herman looked at his glass for a moment.

The bartender gave Adolph an understanding look and pointed towards the door. In his opinion, Herman had had enough.

Adolph took Herman by the arm and started to walk towards Herman's house. It was only two blocks, so Adolph helped Herman up the steps on the porch and into the house.

"I'll see you tomorrow, Herman. Stop over in the evening."

It had been seven years since Adolph's niece had been raped, and all that time Adolph laid off the sex angle with Jeanne, but for the past year Adolph was tossing around in his mind that he'd like to give it a whirl again. He was hesitant thought, because he hardly ever got an erection. His doctor told of a good therapeutic vitamin which he was taking and today was the day he would get his pair of tights that he had ordered on the doctor's advice for his varicose legs.

On the way down to Garden Street where he had ordered the tights, he thought of what Herman had said about the oral sex. Adolph didn't particularly care for it, but . . . . No, he was still thinking he would like to feel the erection and do it that way.

He entered the building and took the elevator to the third floor where the Ajax Supports Supply Co. had their office. The receptionist took his name, and in a few minutes he went into an inner room where he had gotten his fitting. The same girl — the type the guys at the liquor store would say was built like a brick outhouse — who had circled her fingers around his thighs, sort of thrilled him when she took the numerous measurements.

She advised him to keep his shorts on so that the support would not readily soil, and then, because it was such a tight fitting garment, she helped him in straightening out all the creases around the thighs and the crotch.

Adolph let his mind wander, *"Gosh, they were hard to get on. No wonder not many of the senior citizens wore them."*

Not only was it the girl's methodical hand movements that excited Adolph, but it was her beautiful body.

"After a while you'll get the knack of putting them on without any trouble," she said, brightly.

Adolph declared, "I guess if I were an acrobat it would help some."

The girl smiled. "Yeah, I guess you'll be wearing them home?"

Adolph glanced the mirror.. "Yeah, I might as well get used to them." He took his pants from the hanger and put them on.

After getting the tag with the directions for washing and other pertinent information, he paid the ten dollar balance and started for the elevator.

He was proud of the way he looked as he gazed at himself without his trousers, but his mind was racing with screwy ideas . . . no, he couldn't be a homo . . . he liked the females. He was still screwy enough at seven that night to answer the door without his trousers on.

Herman took one look at Adolph's honey-colored tights and said, "Wow!"

"I just got these tights today, and I thought I'd break them in." Adolph was embarrassed and didn't know what else to say.

Herman was still a little unsteady, but followed Adolph into the dining room, then commented. "They look good on you." He then gave Adolph a funny look and added, "Look, Adolph. I didn't have a bite all day. I'll blow you for five bucks."

"How did you get the stuff that makes you walk that way?" asked Adolph.

"I didn't have anything yet. My epilepsy is acting up again and makes me walk this way," snapped Herman.

"Okay, I'll fix you something to eat."

While Adolph prepared some food and something to drink, he thought, *Why not? Herman is thirty years younger so why not see what a younger tool can do.*

Thirty minutes later they were in the bedroom. Herman played around with Adolph's dick for a long while. His tongue got tired, but Adolph's penis remained in a flaccid state.

On the other body, Herman really had a bone on. Adolph took hold of Herman's dick and jerked it off until the juice sprayed. "Your tool reminds me of the way mine was thirty years ago," Adolph stated.

Herman wiped off his organ, then said, "Yeah, but I'm sorry I couldn't get any joy out of your stick. It wouldn't go up."

"That's all right, Herman. You tried hard enough."

They watched television until eleven, then Herman got up to leave, saying, "Don't forget I'm not a professional, not a fairy, but I need the five bucks desperately."

Herman wobbled towards his house that at one time resembled a mansion. Since his father and mother passed away the place was a mess. Windows were shattered, and not replaced, and the house was badly in need of a paint job. As he fumbled with the key in the door he muttered, "I'll be damned if I want to be a dick-sucker."

CHAPTER 10

It was a bright sunny day in June, and Adolph visited his niece.

Adolph said, "Do you notice that almost all of the houses that were for sale were bought by Puerto Ricans?"

Jeanne looked up from her cup of tea. "Yeah, they're doing a good job in fixing them up, too."

Adolph remembered when they weren't sure if they'd stick it out, but they wanted to be near the Holy Fathers Lutheran Church. It was hard to break a tradition.

"I'm afraid I've neglected making some repairs," Jeanne admitted. "I think I should help in sprucing up Pearl Street just as the Puerto Ricans have done."

"What has to be done?" Adolph questioned in surprise.

"Well, for one thing, all the windows need new sashes."

"I'll talk to Herman. He's good at doing that kind of work."

"Herman?"

"Yeah, Jeanne. You know his father was the doctor who had his office right across from the church."

"Oh yes. I remember I went to him for many years. He was a good doctor."

"I did too. I'll see him tonight and tell him you want new sashes put on." Adolph finished his tea..

"That'll be fine. Give him my phone number, and thanks."

"I'll see you later, niece." Adolph kissed her good-bye.

Adolph let Herman in that evening, and they went into the dining room where Adolph brought the bottle to the table.

"I tried to get my TV set working," said Herman. "I've been monkeying around with it for weeks, but it's no damn good."

"We can look at my set later, but first I've got a job for you."

After pouring the liquor Adolph explained. "My niece down the street needs some window sashes." He handed Herman the slip of paper with her address and phone number.

They had downed three shots apiece, and Adolph spoke up. "I don't want you to put your pork in my niece, Herman."

Herman looked shocked, but he said, "I hear you, don't worry. I won't touch her."

"You put the boots to that black girl, and besides, you went down on her meat. I don't want you to try it on my niece," Adolph warned the second time.

"Are you telling me, Adolph, that you never had any black stuff?" He drank the refill and moved closer to Adolph.

"I never had any," Adolph answered.

"Well, maybe you don't have to change your luck."

"That's just it. I might have worse luck, but I don't want any black, yellow or red meat at all."

"All right." Herman was starting to feel his liquor. "You know I'm thirty years younger than you, and I felt like having a piece of ass and the only thing available was black. I don't think I should be hanged, damn it. I didn't negotiate a rape."

"Of course not, Herman, but you know how people think about their relatives."

"No need to worry Adolph. I'm your friend. You helped me lots of times with a shot and a bit to eat, so there won't be any trouble. The job will be done." Herman placed his hand on Adolph's shoulder.

Adolph didn't have anything important to do, so he followed Herman around for the next two days while Herman worked on the windows for Jeanne, without letting Herman see him. It wasn't hard to do because Herman was nearsighted.

He also knew the two men who used to live in Herman's house and hung out in the taproom where Herman liked to drink. He figured after Herman left the taproom, he'd go in and find out if he talked about Jeanne.

By making phone calls to Jeanne's house, Adolph was able to tell when Herman left for the day. Herman left around five and was in the taproom until six. Adolph entered the taproom shortly after six and ordered some vodka. He saw Harry, one of the men that lived in Herman's house, and he walked over to him.

"How are you, Harry?" he asked.

"Okay and you?"

"I'm all right. Did you see Herman today?"

"Yeah. He just left about ten minutes ago," said Harry after a swallow of the suds.

"How's he doing?" Adolph sounded cheerful.

"He just said he's got a job on Pearl Street and he wanted to get back home to clean up."

"That's good. At least he's got a job.

"Yeah. He said he would be finished with the first floor tomorrow and the lady would tell him when to come back to do the second floor."

"Well, good-bye. I'll see you." Adolph waved to Harry.

He went home and waited till Herman had time to eat and shower, then went over.

They sat down in a big room that Herman used for dining and living, and Herman admitted that Adolph's niece was very fussy. "This ought to be like this, and that ought to be like that," he mimicked Jeanne.

Adolph wasn't interested in just chatter. He was waiting to hear something lurid.

After Herman started on his second six-pack, Adolph decided to go home.

The next day, Adolph bought some eighty-six proof whisky to have ready for Herman. He wanted to loosen him up so he might reveal something that night.

First, he called Jeanne and she told him she was glad that he hadn't stopped over the day before because Herman had told her he couldn't work while someone watched. She asked him to wait until the job was done so as not to upset Herman.

Adolph promised to stay away, but at four-thirty he took his post at the corner where he could see Herman coming out of Jeanne's house.

At exactly five o'clock, Jeanne opened the door and Herman came out holding onto his tools, and headed for the taproom. In a half hour, he came out with a six-pack in each hand, evidently leaving his tools to pick up later.

Adolph went in after Herman left, ordered a vodka and hoped to hear something that involved Herman with his niece, but was unable to hear anything. Again, he gave Herman plenty of time to clean up, then he rang the doorbell. This time he asked Herman to come over to his place to watch television.

As the evening dragged on, Adolph brought some cold soda for the chaser. He was anxious to sneak in a few questions, but waited till Herman got a load on.

"Did Jeanne say anything about her love life?" he asked during a commercial.

"No. She only talked about the work she wanted done," Herman answered.

Adolph smiled and poured another drink for Herman. "Didn't she make any suggestions at all?" Adolph was determined to probe the mind of Herman.

Herman moved his tongue across his lips. "Come to think of it, she rubbed up against me a couple of times." He might not have known it, but he was mentally ducking the punches, and on the verge of anguish he let it out. "You know she's not my type, and could never turn me on. She's so darn skinny — got no ass." Suddenly, Herman realized he was talking to Jeanne's uncle and said, "I'm sorry, Adolph." He moved his hand toward Adolph as if to comfort him.

"I forgive you," Adolph said quickly, hoping the matter would be dropped.

Adolph could not dismiss what Herman had revealed to him, and the next afternoon he stopped in to see his niece. Before sitting down, he fulminated, "Herman said you rubbed up against him, Jeanne. What's it all about?"

"Sit down, Uncle, and don't be silly."

"Are you calling Herman a liar?"

"He's probably just kidding you. I did get close to him once when I thought he was going to drop the sash. I was only trying to help. He was so unsteady, but there's nothing to it. You're acting like a jealous child." Jeanne got up and went to the refrigerator. "I've got some beer for you, Uncle."

Adolph calmed down and drank the beer, and when he finished he moved to where Jeanne sat and said, "I'm sorry I said anything to hurt you. Please forgive me." He had no intention of talking to Jeanne about Herman's relation with Marie, the black woman.

"I understand," Jeanne said, giving her uncle a kiss.

Adolph saw Herman many nights during the next year. Herman hardly had any work during that time, and what money he did get, he drank up in booze. They played chess until one night they got to arguing about whether the game was a stalemate or not, then Adolph suggested they play cards. They played gin rummy or pinochle thereafter.

One night after they had their card game and had watched television, Adolph said, "Your boss not only gives you little work to do, but he also wants you to work for peanuts."

"I know, but he knows I can't get any other work," Herman murmured.

"You should become a consultant, Herman. It's like this — a specialist knows a lot about a little, and a consultant knows more and more about less and less."

Herman sat for a moment, shaking the cobwebs out of his head. "Now, I do need a nightcap."

Herman got his drink before he left.

A few weeks later, Herman went to the airport to pick up Rosie, who had just arrived from California. She was going to shack up with Herman again. They were settled in the living room when Adolph showed up to tell Herman his niece wanted him to put in sashes on the second floor.

Adolph was only in the house a few minutes when the doorbell rang. Herman answered it, and ushered his black girl friend into the big room with a sheepish look on his face. He hesitated, then introduced Marie to Rosie and Adolph.

After some verbal exchange, Herman asked Adolph to come into the kitchen to look at a wooden cabinet he had repaired. He then went into a pitch trying to get Adolph interested in the black girl.

"You're not pushing her onto me," Adolph was insistent. "I don't need it."

"You're always talking about pussy," Herman informed.

"I don't remember asking for some black hustler, either."

"Okay, I thought I was doing you a favor. Maybe when she gets to know you, you'll get it free."

As they went back into the living room, Adolph merely shook his head and said, "No, nope."

There was some beer drinking, and later Marie played around with Adolph, but when she asked for fifteen dollars, Adolph rose to say good night.

"Tell your niece I'll be there in the morning," Herman called out.

Adolph had no need to keep track of Herman since Rosie was there, and he saw very little of Herman for about six months. This gave Adolph a lot of time to get acquainted with the neighborhood children.

The Miguel family was the neighbor directly across the street from Adolph. Sylvia Miguel had six boys, ranging from two to seventeen. Her husband was in Chicago, so the family was living off welfare.

Adolph would give the boys a dollar here and there when they helped in the housework, and on occasion some painting.

Ronnie was the one that stopped by the most often. He was sixteen, nice looking and had long hair that came to his shoulders.

Adolph couldn't adjust to their wearing tight pants, and their peckers pointed towards their belly buttons, especially when they watched the young black girls with high asses going by.

Ronnie stopped at Adolphs two nights a week while his mother went to church. On this Wednesday night Adolph was aware that Ronnie was restless, lying on the floor. He was not absorbed in the television show.

"What's bothering you," Adolph asked, noticing the hard outline in Ronnie's pants.

Ronnie hesitated, then said, "I know I can trust you. I needed money for a basketball uniform, and I'm buying a guitar, so I've been letting a kid suck me."

"Is that all?" asked Adolph.

"No. I'd like to try it another way. I want to put it up his rear."

And, now your problem is?" Adolph asked, hiding his bewilderment.

"I want to know if I can get anything doing it that way."

"I guess it's possible, but if everything's clean, you would stand less chance." Adolph turned down the volume on the T.V. set.

"I don't want anybody to know about it because my mom is sending one of us to medical school and I want to be that one."

"You know I won't say a thing," Adolph said, wondering what Ronnie wanted because he was still squirming.

Ronnie saw the puzzled look on Adolph's face and said, "We need a place to do it in."

"We?" Adolph questioned.

"Yeah. Angel and me."

"Who's Angel?"

"Oh, he's something else. You'll like him. He's always got money 'cause his father owns the market at Ninth and Pearl Streets."

"Is his name Torresse?" asked Adolph.

"That's right. They own the Torresse market."

"Let me think it over, Ronnie. I'll talk to you later." Adolph accompanied the boy to the door, and he paused before saying good night and asked, "Don't you go for the girls?"

"Of course," Ronnie smiled. "I'm not gay, but I just want to make some money. He pays me. I don't do it to him."

"Oh," Adolph answered, then added, "See you next week."

Ronnie brought Angel along the next Saturday and introduced him to Adolph. Adolph had to agree that Angel was a cute one.

Angel blushed as Adolph said, "You're a handsome one."

Ronnie walked over to Adolph and whispered in his ear, "You ought to see him . . . ."

Adolph wasn't sure he would like to see the kids in action and wanted more time to think it over. Perhaps it would be of help to him sexually. "Don't forget Ronnie, if I say okay and anything happens you are going to say you only helped me with the housework."

"I promise," and Ronnie crossed his heart.

"I'm going to paint a couple of chairs first, then you can say you did the painting." Adolph advised.

The following Wednesday Ronnie asked Adolph if he could bring Angel around.

"It's all right. I just finished painting the chairs. Don't forget I don't want any trouble."

Ronnie was back with Angel in half an hour, and they were going to use Adolph's bedroom. There was no door between the rooms, but they

68

didn't mind when Adolph sat in the front room and watched them.

Adolph observed, when they took off their clothes, that Ronnie was right. Angel did have a beautiful body. He became more excited when the kids engaged in the act. Ronnie put some spit on the end of his penis before working it into Angel's soft behind.

Angel grunted a little, but he allowed Ronnie to push back and forth until he got satisfied.

Afterwards, Ronnie asked Adolph, "Should we wash up?"

"By all means, wash. Safety first." Adolph showed them to the bathroom.

By the time October rolled around, Adolph was all fired up from the kids maneuvering their bodies around, and he decided to go all out in the physical fitness thing. He asked the doctor about hormones, and the doctor told him they were used mostly by the younger men who had lost their sex drive. The leotards, however, helped in pumping the leg blood back into his heart. Rocking on his toes and heels also helped, and whenever he had to bend he did it from his waist, keeping the support in good shape. Squatting and getting down on hands and knees bunched up the fabric of the support and reduced circulation. The supplier of the support made from surgical material advised against crossing his knees because it would also reduce the circulation. It was, however, all right to cross at the ankles.

Adolph continued to exercise a lot, and he got interested in yoga, read books on the heart and other important functions of the body. All this helped him perk up. He was straighter in body form, and he thought he detected an improvement in the distended penis veins.

After looking in the mirror, he decided he looked good. The leotards did cover an imperfection here and there. He put on his pants.

The doorbell rang, and Adolph let Ronnie in. He noticed a worried look on the boy's face, so he didn't bring out the chess board at this time.

"I've got something to tell you," Ronnie said nervously.

"What is it?"

Ronnie ran his fingers through his hair. "Angel told me he got diarrhea last week, and he blamed it on what I did to him."

"You mean . . . when you had him in bed, Ronnie?"

"Yeah. That's right."

"Is he taking anything for it?"

"Oh, he's not got it now. It wasn't even bad enough for him to take anything, but he said he didn't want me to put any more of the goo in him. He wants me to pull out before I shoot off the next time."

"Well, if I were you I wouldn't bother him any more. He might be allergic to you. Why take a chance on getting involved with Angel that way?" Adolph advised.

"He wasn't angry or anything like that. In fact, I think Angel might be telling a story. Maybe he'd rather suck on me," Ronnie admitted.

Adolph slipped out of his trousers to show Ronnie his leotards.

"Man, you look all right," Ronnie exclaimed.

"Well, you can have me. You won't have to worry about Angel, and I can pay you too," Adolph said without hesitancy.

"But won't you worry Adolph?"

"Not on your life. I'm too old to worry about something like that and besides, I'm going to ask you to pull out before you squirt your load."

Adolph went into the kitchen and came back with a small glass. "See this glass? When you pull out, I'd like you to grab this glass and squeeze your juice in it when you come. You'll have to work fast or you'll lose some of it." Adolph placed the glass on the small table near the bed.

Adolph went on to explain. "I want to measure the difference between the amount you shoot off and the stuff that comes out of my dick."

Ronnie undressed and adjusted everything, topping off his joy stick with saliva and working it in and out of Adolph's old bottom.

The old man had to warn Ronnie to take it easy a couple of times. He had to be satisfied to just put part of his sex organ into Adolph.

It was not long before Ronnie was ready to spout the semen. "I've got it," he shouted.

While Adolph watched, he took the glass and shot into it, squeezing the head of his penis to get it all out.

"Good job, well done," said Adolph as he patted the boy's smooth ass.

They both puffed while getting dressed, and Adolph said, "We'll wait until tomorrow to play a game of chess."

Ronnie took the dollar and went quickly to his home across the street.

Adolph had this quirk of trying to get his thing hard, and he was willing to try anything. What he was about to do was much cheaper than European cell therapy injection where they charged two thousand dollars for eight shots. *And suppose it wouldn't work?* he reasoned.

Adolph took the glass that contained Ronnie's semen and hurried to the medicine cabinet. With a small syringe, he sucked up the semen, then getting hold of his circumcised organ, he squeezed the bulb of the syringe to direct the fluid into his penis. He then pressed the tip of his penis to retain the semen. Using his fingers, he massaged the organ in a backward motion toward his belly.

The job now finished, he relaxed. *The dollar I gave Ronnie was a good investment, and Ronnie had gotten his kicks too,* he thought.

CHAPTER 11

Rosie tried very hard to get Herman to stop drinking and lead a new life, but Herman did not want to get on a company payroll because he was afraid the law would make him pay money to his ex-wife. He blamed his ex-wife for everything that happened to him.

The time came when Rosie couldn't take it anymore. She particularly didn't want to compete with the black girls asking for him. Herman had stopped taking Dilantin for his epilepsy because it relaxed him so much he couldn't be aroused sexually, but stopping the medicine made him agressive and one day in April of 1963 Herman and Rosie fought.

"You're nothing but a stumble bum," she shouted. "You won't work, and all you want to do is drink and screw. Most of the time you can't even get a hard-on, and I'm tired of supporting you. I'm gonna live with my daughter till I get a place."

Herman hollered some incoherent phrases, but wouldn't let go of the beer can he held.

Rosie lost no time in getting out.

That evening, Herman found his way to Adolph's house to tell him about Rosie's departure. After entering Adolph's house, he said, "I need a drink."

Adolph walked to the kitchen to get the bottle. He poured a drink for the shaking man. "So Rosie moved," he said. "Yeah, the schizo beat it. Maybe I ought to be glad. One minute she'd be sucking my cock, and the next she'd be calling me a whoremaster and busting up things."

Adolph took a taste of the whisky, made a bitter face and waved his hand toward Herman, saying, "Well, maybe you can get next to some of that nice Puerto Rican stuff around here."

Herman was silent for a moment then said, "If they didn't live so close and I wasn't afraid to go to jail, maybe I would get into one of them." Adolph poured Herman another drink. He let it slide down his throat, then said, "Ooh, I bet if I put my hand in the snatch of one of those young Puerto Rican girls I would get it burned off."

"That hot?" Adolph laughed.

"What do you think?" asked Herman.

"Yeah, what do you think of Ronnie's mother?"

"Ronnie's mother?" Herman questioned.

"Yeah, she lives right across the street. Ronnie comes over to help me, and I've been teaching him to play chess."

"They live in the brown-front over there?"

"Yeah," Adolph answered.

Herman tongued his lips for the flavor of the schnapps, then said, "She's nice. So's her sister. She was up at my place looking for rooms. She and her four kids are staying at her uncle's house on Ninth Street."

"I guess you weren't thrilled about taking in the kids," commented Adolph.

"Right, and of course, I had Rosie then. The kids could tear up things faster than I could repair them, but the two of them, Ronnie's mother and his aunt have nice round asses." Herman outlined the shape with his hands.

"You like the big woman type, huh," said Adolph. He gave Herman another drink.

Herman knocked the liquor down fast. "Yeah, I like them with plenty of meat. I can see why Ronnie's mother got all those kids."

"She is pretty nice," Adolph agreed.

Herman was dazed and feeling sorry for himself. "I'm no damn good," he cried. "I was the guy picked so that the guys in school could have a smear to look at under the microscope. Yeah, I was the guy that had to jerk off." Herman wavered and blurted, "I even have a hell of a job now when I try to jerk off. I have to use plenty of grease."

"We didn't have anything like that when I went to school," said Adolph. "I don't think we even had a microscope."

Herman lifted his head with difficulty, and his mouth opened with his lips moving, "Speaking of jerking off. When I was in the service I had a pin-up of a beautiful . . . I mean beautiful actress hanging on the wall near my bed. Boy, could I jerk off then. I pulled hell out of my dick, and I did it so good that the actress got pregnant."

Adolph took the bottle back into the kitchen. It was time to lead his rocking friend to the door.

Ronnie saw Angel less frequently as the months passed, and he knew he wouldn't have much time to spend with Adolph. He felt sorry for the old man, and wanted to do something that would make Adolph happy sexually.

Ronnie didn't think Adolph only wanted to measure the stuff he shot into the glass, but suspected that Adolph drank the fluid.

On a cold afternoon in January of 1966, Ronnie had something in mind when he went across the street to say hello.

"You're getting to be a stranger," Adolph said, taking Ronnie's coat to the closet.

"I've got a heavy curriculum, Adolph."

"And a steady girl," added Adolph, raising his eyebrows.

"Oh yeah. I like to take her places."

"To tell you the truth, Ronnie, I'd like to make out with the ladies, but I'm not."

After some thought Ronnie answered, "Look, making time with another guy won't help you with a lady. You might even start to get a high voice."

"I don't know about that, Ronnie."

Ronnie was ready to deliver his message. "You'd do a lot better if you got a young girl and did it to her."

"What am I supposed to do to her?" Adolph inquired.

"Suck her off. See, if you do it to a boy and it makes you girlish, then perhaps if you do it to a girl you'll become mannish. Then you can make out with a lady friend." Ronnie snapped his fingers.

"Do you go to bed with Rosita Torresse, your girl friend?"

"Oh no, Adolph. I intend to marry her, but I used to go with a girl who was pretty hot. Would you want me to ask her?"

"I don't want you to get into any trouble."

"Just leave it to me, Adolph. I'll bring her here and tell her I'm going to do it to her. Then we'll switch. If she gets five dollars I'm sure she'll agree."

"All right, but don't forget you're bringing in your girl. There won't be any lights on, and she must think you're doing it to her. I'll get a bottle of Southern Comfort. You can give her a couple of drinks to make her feel good."

Okay, Adolph. I'll talk to her just as soon as I see her."

They played a game of chess before Ronnie went home.

Ronnie called Elba Banirez the following week, and made a date for the next night.

She was blonde, wore a red coat and gray skirt, and black pumps graced her feet. They met at Broad and Erie streets, then went to see a show at Seventeenth and Chestnut. After the show, they had supper and before Ronnie took her home Elba promised she'd be ready two nights later to go to Adolph's place.

It was already dark when Ronnie brought Elba to the house. He told her he did work for Adolph and in return Adolph allowed him bedroom privileges.

"Pleased to meet you," Elba said sweetly as Ronnie introduced her to Adolph.

Adolph had brought some drinks from the back room, saying, "Help yourselves. I have to straighten up in there."

Ronnie poured the drinks. "This is what you need on a cold night."

Ronnie only had one drink, but Elba liked two and she had that "I don't care if I do" look already.

After a while, they went into the bedroom, closing the door. They were in bed talking and Ronnie knew how to tease her.

"I think I can handle another shot," he said, opening the door to the dining room.

Adolph was already in his pajamas. He slipped them off, and stole into the bedroom. He had to work really fast. The oral performance would have to be finished before Elba wanted to talk.

Adolph finished, then opened the door to let Ronnie back into the bedroom.

Elba, relaxed from the cordial, got her kicks and the job was done so fast she didn't know of the change in personnel.

As they were leaving, Adolph nudged Ronnie and slipped him two fives, saying, "Any time. Good luck to you."

It happened only a few days later that Elba was talking to her girl friend who was a checker in the Torresse Market. There was nobody else in he line, and Elba leaned over the counter and whispered, "Guess who I was with the other night?"

The checker smiled and said, "I give up."

"Ronnie Miguel," Elba answered as though Ronnie was some sort of superstar.

"You don't say."

Right then Elba worked her big mouth to tell Carmen Vasquess, the checker, that Ronnie had gone down on her meat.

Carmen lifted her head toward the ceiling and wondered if Elba knew that Rosita was Ronnie's girl. She soon found out.

Carmen met the boss's daughter on the parking lot at lunch time.

"Rosita, her face aglow, said, "How are you, my dear?"

"Fine, Rosita, and you?"

"Good, Carmen. How's our business?"

"It's terrific on weekends, but a little slow now. Do you know Elba Banirez?"

"I can't say I do," said Rosita.

Carmen then denoted with the news she had heard from Elba.

"Perro sucio," (dirty dog) said Rosita. She followed with so fast a denunciation it was hard to know what she said.

"I know something like that is hard to prove, but I do know Elba is the wild and willing kind. She goes for a lot of sex," said Carmen.

"Carmen, when I see that creep, Ronnie, I'm not handing back the ring, I'm throwing it back." She waved her hand quickly and walked towards the self-opening door of the market.

Rosita later got a call from Ronnie and finally agreed to see him.

Rosita drove the car to a spot on the boulevard where they had been on several dates. Light lunch was served and the juke box blared away. She didn't care for anything to eat, but ordered a Coke. Ronnie ordered a hamburger and coffee.

"You look very sad, Rosita. What happened?"

Rosita sighed, then told him what she had heard.

What could he say? He never finished his sandwich, and Rosita gave back the ring.

There was a wall of silence as Rosita drove to Ronnie's house. She quickly pulled from the curb as soon as Ronnie got out. She didn't even say good-bye.

Ronnie felt like the botton had dropped out of everything. He didn't even feel like studying. As he walked home from school, he met Adolph out walking his dog.

He tried to hide his feelings as he greeted Adolph. "How are you, Adolph?" he asked.

"I'm all right. What's wrong?"

"Oh, you noticed it. I'll tell you after I take my books in the house. " Ronnie leaned over and patted the dog. "I'll see you in a while," he added.

"Okay, Ronnie."

When Adolph answered the doorbell, Ronnie walked to the dining room and sat heavily in a chair. The chess game was all set up ready for a game.

"Where's the little chick?" Adolph asked, wanting to cheer Ronnie up.

"Who? Oh, you mean Elba."

"Yeah," replied Adolph.

"That's why I'm so sad. I want to forget all about her. She opened her big mouth and talked about what happened the other night. She told the checker at the market, and it got back to Rosita." Ronnie lowered his head. "I lost my beautiful Rosita."

"I feel rotten for getting you in this lousy situation," Adolph consoled.

"It was at my suggestion," Ronnie patted Adolph on the shoulder.

"I'm really the dirty old man in this case. I'm at fault for I should never have chanced it."

"There's one sure thing, Adolph. I can't get into any more scrapes for I don't want to lose that scholarship that mom has worked so hard to get."

"Yeah, that's true. We'd better forget about Elba. What do you say? Shall we play a game of chess?"

"Okay," said Ronnie, moving the board in playing position.

CHAPTER 12

Adolph tried really hard to get Herman to stop drinking, or to at least just drink beer, and for a while he did stay off the booze, but it didn't last long. He would get an odd job and buy the liquor again, his excuse being he couldn't stand the screamies. The DT's finally got to him so bad that in the middle of 1969 he had to go to Temple Hospital for treatments.

Ronnie was not seeing Adolph very often for he was in medical school. He needed plenty of books for he was going to be a specialist, so he started working part-time.

With more time on his hands, Adolph called on an old friend, Al Notiso. They used to work together at the liquor store. Al's ambition was to be a foot doctor, but instead of going to medical school he fought in World War I. Because he suffered from shell shock, he received a small pension.

Al drove up to Adolph's house from South Philly, and after Adolph put his fishing gear in, they started towards their favorite fishing spot at Somer's Point in New Jersey.

"I guess all the guys who used to go with us are not around," said Adolph.

"Harry Bowers is the only one left," Al reminded, steering his way.

"Oh, he's the guy who drew a fellow's face on the wall in the men's room at school," said Adolph.

"Ha, ha, yeah. That's the guy — you mean the face with the puffed-out cheeks, and the caption read 'Pregnant Fairy,' " laughed Al.

"Crazy," said Adolph.

"I don't suppose he'll go fishing any more. He's got a thing going for him. He checks all the pay phones and the coin vending machines for money in the return box. He checks in the neighborhood first, then goes up to the Frankford and checks there."

"What a goofy idea," Adolph remarked.

"That's a hobby with him, and sometimes he's lucky, but I'd rather go fishing."

After they arrived at the point, they picked up their things and walked out to the trestle where they liked to fish for flounder. They continued to talk of old times as they sat on the railroad ties.

"Do you still like those Yiddish sayings?" Adolph asked.

"Oh yeah. My favorite is 'Gay cock offin yahm' — translated, it means 'use the ocean as a toilet.' " Al was nuts about Yiddish sayings even though he was Italian. He felt something fighting on his line, so he started to walk towards the bank, saying, "I'm not taking any chances." He meant he wouldn't attempt to pull the fish up on the trestle for fear of losing it.

Al brought the fish slowly to the bank, reeled in the line, and when the fish was on solid ground, he picked up a large stone and hit the fish smack on the head.

"They're not getting away from me anymore," Al shouted.

Adolph shook his head. He'd rather lose one than copy Al's fish-destroying method.

Adolph caught five flounder and Al caught six. After they cleaned them and wrapped them in wax paper, they placed them in a container on some dry ice and placed them in the trunk of the car.

They were riding home on the Pike when a chevy appeared in front of them, moving very slowly.

"I'll tell you what, Adolph. See that slow driver? If that guy ain't smoking a pipe I'll give you my fish."

They pulled alongside the chevy, and there was a gent in his fifties enjoying his pipe, oblivious to the road or to the world. Al did not have to give up his fish.

When Al lined up his Plymouth in front of Adolph's home, he said, "Let's go down again sometime."

"Sure, and thanks a lot."

Herman continued to talk about the rear ends of black girls, and saw Adolph a couple times a week. He still continued to drink, making his epilepsy worse.

Ronnie, however, was unable to visit with Adolph very often. He had a job in North Philly with an electronics firm that helped out college students by allowing them to work four hours out of the two shifts they had going.

He did the same kind of work as some of the girls — running a small press that punched out holes in a bakelite form. Helen Morsan, whose father was the general manager, worked next to Ronnie. Ronnie thought she had to be a main-liner, for she walked like one. He wanted to make a date with her, and after two months finally succeeded.

It was on a Friday evening, and they went in Helen's VW. While Helen drove up the boulevard, Ronnie wanted to know, "Helen, you don't have to work, do you?"

"Not really, but Dad suggested it, and I like the idea. Perhaps if I had a brother, he would not have thought about it."

"He'll know you didn't put in a whole shift tonight," said Ronnie.

"That won't matter. He doesn't mind me dating, especially when I tell him I've been with an employee of the firm.

"Where shall we go?" Ronnie asked.

"Wherever you say," the blonde Helen answered.

"Let me think for a minute." Ronnie's mind was in high gear, then seeing a drugstore, he pointed and said, "Stop here for a minute. I want to get something."

As he moved towards the store he thought of the conversations he had had with Jake, the cabbie who took him to school when he got up late. All he could talk about was sex and about the dose of claps. Ronnie was at the counter and was glad a man would wait on him.

"A pack of Life Savers," Ronnie ordered, then as the candy was on the counter, he said shyly, "Condom."

"We only have the packs of three," said the man.

"Okay."

"Want the three for a half or the dollar pack."

"Three for the half," thinking they should be good enough.

He hurried back to the car and as they were driving, Ronnie offered Helen a Life Saver. "Are you hungry?" he asked.

"No, jus⁺ thirsty."

They were a little past city line when Ronnie said, "Let's stop at this tavern."

From the speaker of the juke box, Ronnie heard, 'I wish you love, I wish you health, but more than wealth I wish you love.' *This was not the place or time to think of Rosita,* he thought.

They later went to a drive-in, and enjoyed the movie. Ronnie got as far as putting his arm around her on that first date.

On the fifth date, he suggested they stop at a motel, to which Helen readily agreed. They registered as Mr. and Mrs., and after watching the small television set, they undressed and laid on the bed. Ronnie took out the rubber out of the pack. He rubbed Helen's belly and felt her ass and his prong got hard enough to easily slip on the condom, then he let her have it.

Helen's belly pumped away and he shot his load, but as he pulled out, he felt for the rubber. It wasn't on his penis.

"Hold still," he said excitedly, "and keep your legs apart until I put on a light." He was worried.

"What's the mat . . . ." but Helen stopped. She felt the object that Ronnie was concerned with.

Ronnie was at her side. "Don't worry. I see it. It stuck in, but I'll get it out."

There was plenty of light for the prospective neurologist, and after reassuring Helen, he reached in for the trapped condom. He retrieved it rather easily from the not so wide receiver. He playfully patted her on the leg as he said, "I didn't need a pair of tweezers." He could smile now, but he wondered what would have happened if he had not been able to get the rubber out.

They dressed and Helen said, "Ronnie, I need a drink."

"I'm all for that," Ronnie agreed, picking up the soggy dick protector which he had wrapped in a Kleenex. He deposited it in the toilet on his way out.

Ronnie and Helen went out together again, but things were different now. Helen insisted, "I don't want you to put one of those things inside me again."

"You don't want to get pregnant, do you?"

"You've heard of the pill, I'm sure." Helen eyed Ronnie.

"I've heard of it, and also of the side effects. I just don't trust it." He was thinking about the cabbie's hard luck when he got the venereal disease.

The couple dated after that, but it was just platonic. Six months later, the firm had a lay-off and Ronnie lost his job. Because of that, Helen would no longer date him, and their lack of interest in each other was mutual.

CHAPTER 13

It was a cold day in February when Adolph learned that Herman was hospitalized again. His boss, who had a key to Herman's house, found him lying on the floor in the living room in a stupor. He called the police, who in turn called the doctor at the clinic. Herman was taken to the hospital, dehydrated.

Adolph recalled that Herman had said one time when he fell in the street from an epileptic seizure plus a drunken state, a nice Bible-reading cop picked him up and took care of him. He got him to a hospital in a hurry and he responded well to the treatment he received.

Herman then said the Lord had been with him, and he started to read the Bible.

Adolph, thinking he was getting too far apart with his sex hang-up, reading all that sex literature and taking ginseng, etc., wanted a change of pace. For a while his imagination led him to believe he was getting better with a bed job, but with all his maneuvering and conniving, his performance was not any better.

Consequently, Adolph sat in the living room reading the Bible — the chapter where Aaron made the golden calf, and the Lord was good to Adolph also.

The paper boy threw in the newspaper on this Thursday, the day when the winning lottery numbers were published. Adolph took out his ticket from the bureau drawer and placed it in the Bible opened to the chapter he had just read.

Suddenly, he cried out with laughter. "Lord Almighty. I hit." His frame shook and in his attempt to jump, his feet hardly left the floor. He drank a shot of vodka and got set to visit his niece.

"Here's the ticket, Jeanne. See if I got a winner."

Adolph sat on the edge of the chair in the front room.

"Goody goody, gum drops, are you ever lucky!" Jeanne said. "You've got the winning number and the number that doubles the prize. A hundred thousand." She gave her uncle a long affectionate kiss.

"The trouble is, we can't let everybody in this neighborhood know I won all that money, or I'd have a con man and his brother after me."

"Well, it's going to be tough, and I doubt whether you can stop people from knowing about it, but why don't you see Martin?"

"Yeah. I'll see your brother. Maybe he will have a good idea." Adolph was relieved.

"Give him a call on Saturday. He'll most likely be home, and when you see him, give him my love."

"I'll do that, Jeanne. I hope he's home because I plan on seeing Herman at Temple Hospital on Sunday.

"How is Herman?"

"He's getting better. I called him just last night."

"Tell me how you make out with Martin."

"Right, and here's a good night kiss, Jeanne."

"Good night, uncle."

Adolph looked at the lottery ticket again and again before going to see his nephew in Levittown. He got on the bus, and from the Levittown station, he took a taxi to 247 Sunset Lane where his nephew lived. Everything looked so neat, making him aware of the difference between his part of town and where his nephew lived.

After showing Martin the winning ticket and explaining the problem, Martin said, "You can't keep a big prize like this a secret."

"Right, Martin, but I'm sure that if I get the ticket validated in the liquor store in my neighborhood, I'm in for trouble."

"If you get it validated in any store, people will still know about it." Martin got up from the large chair in the living room, and added, "Hold on. I think I can save you some money."

Martin switched on the stereo to play some soft music, then went to a bookcase where he kept the manuals which helped him in his work as an accountant in the income tax field.

"The tax bite is pretty heavy on this amount," he said. "Almost half if you report the whole amount on your return, Adolph. Now let me figure this out."

Martin worked again on the tax table, then said, "It's like this. I can get the ticket validated, then report the income split three ways — between you, sis, and me. Our tax then will be roughly one thousand a piece. When I give you my net, twenty-three thousand, you will have forty-six thousand and sis will have twenty-three thousand. That will be twenty-three thousand dollars more in the family than if you reported all the income on your return."

"You'll have to get something for your trouble, Martin."

"That's all right, Uncle. I won't take anything from you."

Adolph thought it over, then said, "I'll let Jeanne keep the twenty-three thousand."

"You don't really have to let her have it all," Martin advised.

"An you take five thousand for yourself, Martin."

Martin paused before he said, "I'll be satisfied with a thousand. I won't take a penny more."

"We'll shake on that," Adolph said, extending his hand.

Adolph entered the Broad Street entrance of Temple Hospital Sunday afternoon, and took the elevator to the fourth floor where the psychiatric ward was located. He found Herman in Room 427, and he looked all right. He had his hair cut, was clean shaven and wore clean pajamas.

Adolph didn't feel like telling Herman about the lottery ticket for fear he would talk about it when he was in the taproom.

"You're looking good, Herman. How do you feel?"

"I'm all right now. How are you?" Herman answered.

"Okay, I didn't know what to bring you so I have a box of non-chocolate covered candies for you. I hope you like them."

"Thanks," Herman said as the nurse came in to take his temperature.

"Temperature and pulse okay," she smiled. "Don't go away. I'll be right back."

Herman focused on the white pantyhose of the nurse as she left the room. "I'd like to intrude my joy stick into that," he said.

"That's a fine way for a Bible-reading man to talk," said Adolph.

"Bible? Did you read about Lot's daughters?" Herman asked.

"Yeah, and I guess you read about the flood," countered Adolph.

"Yeah," said Herman, letting his mind wander. "You know I must be slipping. The first time I was in here I picked up a crazy girl. Now I can't even do that."

"When are you going home?"

"The doctor said he'd let me know next week. How's everything around your place?"

"All right."

The nurse came back with Herman's chart. She asked several questions, jotting down the answers. "You'll live," she said cheerfully. "Don't forget to buzz if you need anything."

Adolph sat alongside of Mrs. Miguel at Ronnie's graduation from medical school. Her eyes sparkled when Ronnie received his diploma. Ronnie walked with the familiar mortar outfit and gave his mother a kiss, then after the exercises were over, Adolph took Ronnie and his mother to a nice place on the Boulevard where they had refreshments.

As they parted, Adolph said, "Don't forget to stop around tomorrow. I've got something for you, Ronnie."

The next day Adolph gave Ronnie a portable typewriter.

"I never expected this kind of gift," said Ronnie.

"I won some money in the lottery, so I can afford it. I'm glad you will be able to use it."

"Thanks a lot, Adolph." Ronnie was smiling.

"I made you lose your girl friend, Ronnie, and I think it's my duty to help you whenever I can." Adolph rose from the chair and placed his hand on Ronnie's shoulder.

Ronnie got up. "I don't want you to think you owe me anything. We'll just have to forget the incident." Ronnie lowered his eyes, realizing some things were not so easy to forget.

"Yeah, you're right, Ronnie. Have a drink?"

"No thanks. I want to get up early and see about a job. You know I'm waiting for an internship so I'm just getting a temporary job until I get it."

Ronnie worked the four to eight p.m. shift at I.R.S. until the hospital called for him. The I.R.S. was giving the college students a break, just the same way the North Philly electronic firm did where Ronnie worked for six months.

The supervisor introduced him to the key personnel in the Files Department. The aisles were very narrow, in order to conserve space, and Edie Miles rubbed up against him. She wore a deep purple short dress and black pantyhose, and made Ronnie hot on his first day of work. In a short while, he had to go up the same aisle for a document. This time Edie was dragging a chair along with her. She placed it in the middle of the aisle, plunked herself on the seat and wrapped a splendid leg around her other one and looked at Ronnie.

Ronnie wondered whether she was doing all that for his benefit, and he soon found out.

Still looking up at him, she simply said, "I'm going to screw you." She then turned her head away.

Ronnie was talking to Randy Ross the next week. Next to breathing, Randy liked to talk the most. He showed Ronnie pictures of his girl friends.

"See this one," he pointed to a girl. "She's easy to hypnotize."

"Did you go to school to learn?" asked Ronnie.

"No, I just picked it up from reading books." Randy had the appearance of a stage hypnotist with the penetrating eye, the hair combed to a point on his forehead, parted mustache, bearded chin and long slender fingers.

"Did you ever try it on Edie Miles?"

"That nut? I can't hypnotize the screwballs."

"You know what she said to me?" asked Ronnie.

"What did the nut say?"

After listening to Ronnie's explanation, he said, "She'll say something like that to any guy. She's a loose wrap if there ever was one," Randy observed.

"Say Randy, I wonder whether it's possible to hypnotize a girl into doing a sex act?"

"I guess if she was the kind who would do it without hypnotism," explained Randy.

"Otherwise no?"

"Exactly. The straight-laced girl would still not comply. She simply would not spread her legs even under a spell."

"Have you been working on this job very long?" Ronnie asked.

"Five months, but I expect to get a better job in Washington soon. I'm waiting for a vacancy."

"I hope you get it soon. What was your school?"

"U of P, 1968, and yours?"

"The same, but 71 for me. I'm waiting for an opening in a hospital. I just want to make a few bucks in the meantime."

The lunch bell rang, and Ronnie and Randy walked up the big aisle towards the cafeteria. Randy pointed to a very tall man in the crowd.

"That's Bob," he explained. "He always carries a chess board. Nobody beats him. He taught chess when he was younger. Do you play, Ronnie?"

"I know the moves, but I'm not very good," Ronnie admitted.

"Maybe you ought to do what Bob does. He's a food nut, vitamin addict and goes in a big way for peanut butter — the kind made with raw peanuts. If you want to find him in the aisles, it's easy. Just follow the odor of peanut butter," Randy smiled.

The next day a blonde was looking for a document in the same area where Ronnie and Randy were working. After watching her stretch to get a folder from the top shelf, Ronnie said, "Is yours rising too?"

"She can make it bristle," commented Randy. "She's got a grade five already. She's going places in the examining department."

"Grade five?" Ronnie questioned. "That's $150 a week!"

"Right — the chief of the department has her for a pet."

"How old is he?" Ronnie asked.

82

"He must be close to fifty. They say he goes down on her pussy."

Ronnie laughed. "That pussy's good, but sometimes it's hard to separate fact from fiction."

"Yeah," said Randy. "Some of the whites might be over-reacting because the chief is black."

Ronnie worked just a few days beyond three weeks at the I.R.S. department when he was given an assignment at Temple Hospital. Dr. Ronaldo Miguel was now an intern.

Right up to the Spring of '72, Dr. Miguel looked at many cases in the hospital. He found that the nervous tunic of the eye was not a disease — it was the retina. He also learned that a cut nerve could be sewn and restored in six months to two years. As a specialist, he got experience in the nervous system. Every movement of the body depended on it. It is what signals the brain so that things can be seen by the eye.

Dr. Miguel became very adept at reading electroencephalograms. He interpreted the spikes which are very sharp waves in the temporal parts. He had a keen interest in brain patterns of people with epilepsy.

CHAPTER 14

Herman was home from the hospital, and Adolph went over to see him. When he received no answer to the doorbell, he knocked loudly. The kitchen window was open, and Adolph knew Herman wouldn't leave it open if he had gone out. The shades were up and Adolph heard a radio playing.

Suddenly, a whiff of urine came from the window, and Adolph became alarmed. He stood on the corner, and after waiting ten minutes a police car appeared. He flagged it down, and they were able to get into the kitchen.

The cop found Herman in the big room. He had fallen off the sofa and was lying on the floor. On the table was a medical book opened to a page and resting on a Bible. The cop read the page. It explained intoxication and anti-convulsant drugs — the sleepiness, the stupor and then the coma from which there could be no awakening. It looked as if Herman was trying to commit suicide.

"Was he always reading these kinds of books?" the cop asked.

"He read a lot of medical books, only because his father was a doctor and left a lot of them."

The cop radioed for the emergency van, and it arrived in about ten minutes.

Adolph followed the van to the hospital, and met his friend, Dr. Miguel. There was a resident doctor there also, Dr. Sergio Santos.

The cop showed the book opened to the page on the anti-convulsant drugs to Dr. Santos.

After the doctor read the page, he said, "This page is about an overdose of drugs. Is this man an epileptic?"

"Yes, doctor, he is," said Adolph.

"Do you know what he was taking for it?"

"He mentioned Dilantin to me a long time ago," Adolph said.

"There's no known antidote against any of the anti-convulsant drugs — we'll have to work fast," the doctor advised.

Adolph looked beggingly at the doctor. "Bring him around. Don't spare the expense. I have the money."

Herman's pulse rate was slowing as the doctor told the orderly to wheel in the dialysis machine. "There's definitely no time for substitutional transfusion," he declared.

The machine was hooked up to the membrane lining of the abdominal wall. Both doctors watched carefully as the modern process was eliminating the drug overage by passing the lower molecular weight substance, but preventing the dispersion of the higher molecular weight matter.

All of his life signs and pulse were soon getting back to normal, and in twenty minutes Herman opened his eyes. Dr. Miguel told Adolph that he would be in a fog for sometime. "Do you want to call tomorrow? He'll be able to talk to you then, Adolph."

"Will he be all right?"

"Oh yes. He'll be fine."

"Tell him not to worry about the bills. I've been lucky, so I'll take care of the bills."

"Okay, I'll tell him. You're very kind, Adolph."

"Well, I owe it to him. So long, doctor. I'll see you tomorrow."

Adolph visited Herman on Friday.

"You should never have tried to leave us, Herman," said Adolph.

Herman nodded, and paused. "See, I was a failure again."

"Don't let anything worry you, Herman. You're young and have plenty of mileage left. Dr. Miguel is my friend, and I told him I'd pay your bill."

"Nonsense. Why should you have to pay my bill?"

"I owe you. Some years ago when you worked on my niece's house, I poured liquor down your throat to try to get you to talk." Adolph turned his head away for a moment.

"Oh, that," Herman laughed. "You got it wrong. When we weren't together I drank plenty of liquor. You weren't responsible for my drinking. I thought it was doing me good, and I felt better." Herman placed his hand in Adolph's. "Don't make me cry, Adolph. Thousands of times I felt like it, but my father used to say, 'We're Germans — we don't cry.' "

"All right, Herman, don't cry. You'll make me feel bad. Just do what the doctor says and let me take care of the bill or else I'll cry."

I'll try hard, Adolph. Notice I'm not drinking," Herman laughed.

"Yeah. When you get out of here just pretend you're still in the hospital and not allowed to drink."

"Yep, I'll have to change my way of living," Herman remarked.

Just then Dr. Miguel entered the room. "How's the patient?" he asked.

"All right," Herman answered.

"You look much better. We worried about you." The doctor felt Herman's pulse. "Okay, Herman."

"Thanks to you, doctor."

"What kind of work do you do?" the doctor asked.

"Carpentry," Herman replied.

"That kind of work can get tough."

"I know. I get so tired after two hours work I have to take a rest, but in my condition I'm lucky to get any kind of work."

Dr. Miguel took a couple cards from his pocket and handed them to Herman and Adolph. "I'm opening an office at Twelfth and Pearl Streets next Monday. When you're released I want you to come to my office." The doctor moved closer to Herman. "Don't forget. No more liquor. The medicine won't work right if you drink, and another thing, I'm going to try to get you some lighter work until you get on your feet."

"I'll do just as you say, Doc. I know you're doing a lot for me, and I appreciate it."

The doctor left the room just as the nurse entered.

"How do you feel?" she asked.

"Getting along good," said Herman.

After the nurse left, Adolph spoke up. "I didn't see you looking at her rear end. Are you slipping, Herman?"

"I already slipped. It's time for me to think of the front end at the top of my head." Herman clarified by pointing to his forehead.

"A cool head and a warm bosom, as one of our customers at the store used to say," Adolph commented.

"Not bad," Herman replied.

"Good-bye for now, Herman. Don't miss any visits to the doctor when you get out of here, and no more booze."

Herman was out of the hospital in eight days. He walked steadier than he had for years. He wore a blue serge suit and black oxfords that Wednesday in May as he rang the bell outside the doctor's office. He opened the door and entered the waiting toom.

When it was his turn, the receptionist told Herman to get on the scales. She marked down his weight on the card. The doctor then greeted Herman with a big smile. "I've read your latest report from the hospital and it shows remarkable improvement. You were on a high fat diet at the hospital, and for medicine we alternated with Luminal and Butisol. All you'll need now is this." He wrote the prescription for Luminal.

"Take one of these when you feel shaky. You know the feeling."

"Indeed I do," Herman answered.

"You won't need anything else. Just the Luminal. Now I'd like to tell you about a job I think you'll be interested in. I have a friend who is a superintendent at the Rolling Cab Company, and he said there's an opening. If you pass the test, everything will be okay."

"I'll have to take a driver's test first because I didn't renew my license in over two years," Herman said.

"Take the test. I'm sure there'll still be an opening when you pass."

"I'd like to try it. Thanks, Doc."

"That's okay. The fresh air will be good for you, and it's an easy job. Here's a card to take with you. Good luck."

Herman applied for a permit, took the test and passed. It was almost summertime when his driver's license arrived in the mail.

He went to the office on a June morning and showed the card the doctor had given him. He clerk at the desk allowed him into Mr. Gill's office.

Mr. Gill, the supervisor, gave Herman an application which he filled out. He was then told to report the next day for a company driving test.

The instructor took Herman into the center of town, then let him drive. Herman did all the correct things like driving at the proper speed and applying the brakes at the right time. The instructor said he passed with flying colors.

Herman stopped by Adolph's the next week to have a chat with him. He told Adolph he got the job.

"How are you doing on it?" Adolph asked.

"Fine."

"Good tips?"

"They'll be better next week when I get night work," said Herman.

"You get the big spenders then, huh?"

"Yeah, the jobs are different," acknowledged Herman.

"How about the cat houses?"

"There's some of that from what I hear the drivers say, but listen to this gem. You'll never believe anything like it could happen in broad daylight."

"Let me bring out some soda first, Herman. I know you're off the hard stuff," Adolph suggested.

Herman took a large drink of ginger ale, then started the tale. "It was nine in the morning when I picked up a couple at Fifth and Berks. They had just come out of a tap room. He was a thin, young guy and she was a thin old lady. He told me to drive to Thompson Street where there was a big lot. The houses had been torn down five years earlier, and when we got there he asked me to take a walk after sticking a five in my hand. Well, I complied. When he was ready, he leaned on the horn and I got into the cab to drive them to Front and York." Herman took another drink of the soda, then continued. "Only the lady got out there. After she went up the El steps, the guy turned to me and said, 'See that old lady? She gave me the best piece of ass I ever had.' "

"I didn't know what to say, and finally I got out a huh, huh. The guy went on, 'I think she thought it might be her last.' He looked at me with wide open eyes and told me to drop him off at a bar a few blocks to the north."

Adolph sneaked in a little of the hard stuff with his soda, drank some of the mixture and then said, "I'm not sure I'm interested in that porno."

"What's bothering you, Adolph? That's not porno, it's life."

"Yeah, I guess I ought to write off sex. I'm not getting to first base with it," complained Adolph.

"What's buggin' you, Adolph? You can't turn off life on account of a sex hang-up. Do you think my sex life is flourishing? I'm not finding any wet, sticky material on the inside of my pants."

Adolph smiled. "But you got a lot of mileage left. I'm practically on my last legs."

"I hope not, Adolph. You've been good to me, and your kindness had been a big help in my doing much better."

Adolph drained the glass of soda. "Well, I'm glad about that. I hope you keep picking up. Let's see what's on TV."

"Okay. There might be something good on."

Herman got the twelve to nine in the morning shift the following week. He was feeling better all the time, and he even looked better. He still shook his head, but not as much as formerly, and he was more expressive. He liked people talking to him — it encouraged him and they were giving him better tips. He held the graveyard shift until a week before Christmas, then he was put on the noon to nine shift.

He stopped in to see Adolph, and asked, "How are you?"

"Not so hot," Adolph replied.

"Cheer up. It's near Christmas." said Herman.

"Christmas is for kids." He walked to the dresser and took an envelope from a drawer. "I want you to be sure and see that your kids get this."

"What's in there?" said Herman, surprised.

"Fifty bucks. I want to give the kids a break."

"Thanks, Adolph, but I don't want you to go overboard."

"No I'm not going overboard. You know I won the lottery."

"Yeah. I'll make sure the kids get it. They'll have the best Christmas yet." Herman grabbed Adolph's hand and shook it.

Herman was very busy working, and didn't have time to see Adolph until Christmas day when he went over and exchanged gifts with him. He was also very busy before New Years, but he did take time out to watch the Lombardo show with Adolph.

On January tenth, he went on the midnight shift again. The happenings were bizarre. The first one was when he picked up a black man who told him to take him to a bar at Tenth and Wood Streets.

"Come on in," the passenger said. "It's on me."

"Sorry, I can't drink — Doctor's orders." Herman said, but he followed the fellow into the tap room. He hadn't been paid yet.

His fare ordered a drink of V.O. The bartender, a white man, husky, hippyish and with a lot of hair and mustache, waited for the money.

"You know Flo Davis, don't you?" asked the black patron. He was a heavy-set man with a mustache. He wore a tan overcoat with a fur collar.

The bartender's face turned red, and he said, "All right."

Herman's fare got another drink before walking back with Herman to the cab. When the wheels pulled away from the curb, the guy told Herman how he got free drinks.

"I happen to know the bartender puts the boots to Flo Davis, a cute black chick who is married. All I have to do is order the booze and ask, 'How's Flo.' I get free stuff. I don't give a damn whether he puts any money in the register or not for the drinks." The passenger laughed. He must have felt pretty good about the whole thing.

Herman was not so fascinated with the idea. He considered it a dirty blackmail job.

The next week Herman had a pickup at Tenth and Vine. The guy was feeling no pain, but felt like talking and told Herman a story about some old guys who were trying to get a boost out of their dicks, just like Adolph tried to do.

"You know, pal," the pickup said. "I work for the railroad. We get around the sub-stations, the ones that have the electrical equipment. We do the maintenance work. Well, anyhow, I used to see these young girls come out of Beacon College which is right near our Newton substaion. These girls would hand the old guys something, and the old geezers would give them money. I never knew what it was all about until a railroad dick told me. He said the girls were selling their urlne. They called it maiden's piss."

Herman reached the destination. "What do you think of them old geezers?" asked the fare.

"Very freakish," said Herman. "But I don't know any law against it."

The fare fumbled around in his pocket looking for his wallet. "That's just what the railroad cop said, but can you imagine anybody drinking piss?"

"Not even with orange juice," said Herman.

The passenger paid Herman and handed him a quarter tip. "Maybe you'd rather have a fifth of maiden piss for a tip."

"No thanks. I don't drink," said Herman, getting in his cab and pulling away from Tenth and Fairmount.

CHAPTER 15

Harry Springer first met Mildred Boyd when they were going to high school. They dated, fell in love and were married in 1952. They lived in a rented house in the lower part of Kensington until Harry got a steady job at the Post Office. After working there for two year, they placed a down payment on a piece of property in Upper Kensington. It was a nice brick front house near the shopping center. Mildred and Harry were happy there.

Their son, Ralph, was born in 1954, and Harry finally got ambitious. He started to write numbers on the side, and he got players where he worked and also at the newsstand on the corner.

By 1957 he got greedy. He wasn't satisfied with fifteen percent — he wanted the eighty-five, so he decided to bank the numbers. If the play was too heavy he gave the surplus to a friendly number writer. He was lucky. He could cover all the hits and the law didn't bother him. The ward leader was his friend.

Business was wonderful and Harry wanted to show his female writers he had class. He bought a home on the Main Line, near Fairmount Park. Harry became more suspicious of outsiders and wouldn't hire help to help Mildred. When he threw a party for the big bookers, Mildred did all of the cooking and washing and cleaning, besides taking care of Ralph who was ten years old. Two years after they bought the Main Line home, Harry started chasing women. In the following six years, Mildred worked so hard that Harry finally got some help. He opened up his heart and had a female writer help her.

Starting in 1970, Mildred had trouble remembering things. Ralph, who was eighteen, was the first to notice how his mother would peer at the newspaper to see what day it was. She couldn't concentrate, and her shopping lists were always mixed up.

Harry decided to entertain at one of the big restaurants, giving him a chance to do a lot more cheating. Instead of trying to help his wife, he ignored her. Mildred finally retreated into a world of her own and did a lot of staring.

It was late in 1972 when Harry came home from a long trip, and he found Mildred walking around as thought she had lost something. She was looking all through the living room.

"How are you, Mildred?" he asked.

Mildred stared at him a moment, then said, "I'm all right. Isn't everyone?"

"Are you looking for something?" asked her husband.

"I couldn't find a box of tea," she explained.

"You're kidding. You know the tea bags are always in the kitchen." Harry walked toward the kitchen.

Mildred watched Harry's lips move, then she laughed. "What do you know. That's right. In the kitchen." She went into the kitchen and found them.

Harry was worried and knew she needed a doctor. "If you don't feel well, I can call a doctor," he said. "I can drive you over to see

Dr. Beardsley in Kensington. You liked him."

Don't bother. I don't need a doctor. Mildred giggled and looked at the newspaper. "Oh, it's Tuesday. I thought it was Monday," she said aloud.

Harry remembered she had said the same thing before he went on his trip. He waited no longer. He went out to his car to drive to Dr. Beardsley.

Mildred was standing near the wall, looking at a calendar.

On account of a convention in town, Herman was given the six p.m. to three a.m. shift. He was stationed at Broad and Vine when Mildred Springer approached.

"Have you seen Harry?" she asked.

"I haven't been on the cabs very long. I don't think I can help you, lady," he answered.

Mildred giggled. "He lived in Kensington, and we played hide the weenie."

Herman saw a frivolous woman who he thought was on the make. He looked again. She was built pretty good, and since he hadn't had anything for a long while, he thought he could give her a dig.

"I know how to play that game too," he said.

Mildred kept on giggling as the wind caught her short red dress.

"Would you like to come over to my place?" he asked.

Mildred nodded in agreement. The poor overworked woman was dreaming of her good life in Kensington, but now her thoughts and actions were disembodied.

Herman took her to his house, and they had something to eat.

"Where do you live?" Herman asked.

"Harry's coming with my clothing. We're going to live in Kensington," she said as though she were in a trance.

Herman suspected that Harry had picked her up, but he would like to try and get her to shack up with him instead.

"Want to stay here for a while," he asked. "I'll get you some clothes in the morning."

She giggled and nodded.

Before leaving, Herman made her comfortable, sitting her alongside the TV set, and told her to wait until he got through work. "If you want anything to eat, just open the fridge," he said.

Herman locked the front door and went back to his cab, and when he returned home the next morning, he found Mildred still sitting, and giggling with the TV on. She wiggled on the sofa.

"It's Tuesday," she said leaning over to read the date on the newspaper that was lying on the sofa.

"Well, it's really Wednesday now, early in the morning," Herman explained. "I'll make some tea for us, then we'll hit the hay."

After they crawled into bed, Herman felt like cursing. He had it in front of him, and here was his chance of getting something without beating his meat, and he couldn't get it hard.

I'm getting bad as Adolph, he thought, *but he's thirty years older. Maybe I need vitamins or something.*

Mildred was submissive and Herman, for the time being, didn't realize that it wasn't Rosie in bed with him. He put his dick up against her lips. He wanted her to open her mouth.

Mildred began to sob, saying, "I never did this with Harry."

Herman put his arm gently around her, saying, "Don't cry. I'm sorry. Let's go to sleep." Herman hoped that he would be better the next day.

In the morning, he took her over to the Avenue and bought her some clothes. When they came back, they prepared to eat. Mildred stood up to help. She put a spoon of percolated grind in the cup and added hot water.

"No, Mildred," Herman said. "Use this." He showed her the instant.

It was afternoon now and Mildred grabbed the dishes and started doing them up. Herman noticed she lined everything on the table in a very neat fashion. She seemed to function correctly while working on the dishes, but Herman suspected that everything wasn't right on her top floor. Being a doctor's son, he decided to help her. Before going to work, he dirtied all the dishes he owned so Mildred would have some wok to do.

"Take your time on the dishes," he advised her. "I'll see you later." Herman gave Mildred a kiss before going to work.

CHAPTER 16

Alex Cortez was born and brought up in the same neighborhood that Dr. Miguel was. There were a lot of boys in the Cortez family, seven in fact. They all lived with their mother in a small house on Wallace Street, just south of Pearl Street. That one lousy toilet for all of them had to be one of the reasons the kids left home.

Alex was seventeen when he married a girl who was fifteen. The marriage lasted only two years. His wife packed up and took the two kids after Alex got into the dope racket.

Alex then worked in a hospital, supermarket and was presently employed in a drug supply house. The grass was easy to get, but when he got on the heroin bounce, it was harder to get, besides it was more expensive. He needed more and more money to support his kicks.

He belonged to the fast crowd. None had excess flesh, especially the girls. Their bodies were built for moving, and move they did. The speed of the group could be killing, but Alex played it smart. He'd take a hiatus, hide for a while and dream. He'd go to work in a half-awake condition from the small doses of barbituates he stole.

When he jerked out of the dream, he'd go back to his gang and spend his money on dope, girls and hitting the night spots. He also spent a lot of time dreaming and scheming about a beautiful way of getting a lot of money. He knew Michael Torresse owned four super-markets, and he wouldn't want that beautiful daughter, Rosita, harmed. He had seen the girl many times when he worked in the market.

Alex looked in the mirror and saw a light-complexioned angular face, a head with long, black wavy hair, and his chin was dimpled. He had long sideboards close to his small ears.

He considered himself as good looking as any of the Spanish speaking fellows in the neighborhood. He knew several who had married either an Irish girl or a Polish girl, and he was determined to show those pussy bumpers a thing or two when he got a bundle. He would get an Irish or Polish girl for himself.

He knew the Torresse girl used to show at the market between five-thirty and six. He had gone to the parking lot on Monday and Tuesday, but the girl didn't show up.

On Wednesday, in the middle of February, he opened the drawer of his dresser and took out a .38 caliber gun. He also picked up a sodium pentathol needle he had stolen from the supply house where he worked. Using some of the knowledge he obtained from the time he worked in the hospital, he took a plastic bottle. Next he put a ball of absorbent cotton in a saucer, poured alcohol over it, and placed the needle point up in the bottle. He then laid the cotton on top. The needle would be sterile for use.

At a quarter to six, he saw Rosita park her compact car on the lot of the Torresse Market. She was stepping out of the car wearing a short denim coat and beige panythose.

A hand under the sleeve of the black raincoat was placed tightly against her mouth with a warning, "Don't say a word, or I'll kill you."

A blue Impala came up alongside of the compact. Alex quickly opened the door on the driver's side and in a low threatening voice commanded, "Come on, now. Get out fast. Leave the motor running or I'll blow your brains out."

The driver was terrified, but got out of the car.

Alex worked fast. He slipped down the pantyhose of Rosita who was in a state of shock, too frightened to scream, and jabbed the sodium pentathol needle into her thigh. He then pushed her into the back of the Impala and jumped into the driver's seat.

The one-way traffic forced Alex to drive past the security guard. The guard drew his pistol and shot at an angle into the windshield. The bullet ricocheted and struck Alex in the right arm near the shoulder. He held onto the wheel with his other hand and stepped on the gas, and turned out of the field of the guard's fire.

The pain was getting to be too much for Alex, so he stepped on the brake just a few doors from Dr. Miguel's office. He didn't know if that was the day for office hours, but decided to take the chance. He rang the doorbell.

The doctor was in the inner room where he was preparing to take an EKG on a patient.

"Would you mind helping me with a lady?" asked the kidnapper. Alex led the doctor to the blue car.

"Rosita Torresse!" exclaimed the doctor. "What's happened to her?"

"Let's get her inside, then I'll explain everything."

They carried Rosita into the doctor's office and laid her on the table in back of a partition where women patients undressed.

The abductor showed the doctor his gun. "She's all right. She's just sleeping. I gave her a needle, but I want you to take a bullet out of my arm, and no slip-ups." He waved the gun toward the doctor with a menacing look. "I'll be watching every move so don't try to pull a fast one. I've had experience in hospital work. Don't give me a general. I'll take a local you know, like Novocain, and don't forget if I feel myself going to sleep, I'll give you a bullet right in the brain, and I might just get a shot at the girl."

Dr. Miguel thought for a while there was a way to outsmart the bum, but he gave up the idea. He would do what the thug wanted. Alex looked like a nut, anyway.

"Let me look at that first," Alex said, taking the bottle from the doctor. "Yep, I can read. It's Novocain so go ahead," he said.

The doctor applied the anesthetic, then tested the area where the bullet had lodged. "Any feeling here?" he asked.

"No. It's numbed," Alex answered. He thought the doctor was stalling, so shouted, "Come on man, and get the lead out." Again he flashed the gun.

"Here, take these first," the doctor said as he gave him two tablets with a glass of water.

"What are they?" Alex asked.

"Don't worry. They're not sleeping pills. They're sulphanilamide, to prevent infection. You didn't want any needle."

Alex swallowed the medication, and repeated the earlier threat.

Dr. Miguel scraped the wound first, then cut to get the bullet out. It was easy to get. There could be no subterfuge in the operation, and any attempt would be a dismal failure.

"I could have scooped it out myself," the kidnapper laughed. "That's if I was left handed and wanted to be charged with practicing without a license, eh, Doc?"

Dr. Miguel affixed the bandage and had almost everything cleared from the table when the bell rang.

Alex wore his scowl again. "If it's the cops, send them away," he snarled.

The doctor gathered the rest of the material and put it in the back of the screen, then went to the door.

"Yes," he said.

"Sorry, Doctor, but there's a stolen car out front and we're checking. There's been a kidnapping too," said the cop.

"Everything's all right here," said the doctor.

"Okay, just routine. Goodnight." The officer left.

When the doctor returned to his desk, Alex said, "You must like the chick a lot, but I will say you were good, Doctor." Alex pointed to the screen. "I hear a noise. I think she's getting up."

Alex picked up the phone and cut the wire where it came out of the receiver. Holding the wire in his hand, he said, "Doc, see if the chick is awake, and if she is, tell her to keep quiet and do what I tell her."

Dr. Miguel walked behind the screen and found Rosita fighting the sodium pentathol out of her system.

She recognized Ronnie, but he quickly warned her to stay quiet.

"Where am I?" she whispered.

"You're in my office. A crazy man has kidnapped you, and your best bet is to do what he says or he might kill you. He has a gun. I can't say any more."

Alex called out, "Come on now, no love festival." He looked around at the three doors. The door on the other side of the room opened to Twelfth Street, and Alex wanted to take his hostage through that one.

"Show me how to get out this door," he said. "You can let go of her hand now."

The doctor showed him how the door opened, then Alex pushed him to the radiator and tied him there with the telephone wire. He grabbed the horrified girl. "Come on, sister, you won't get hurt as long as you're quiet." He put the gun in the coat pocket.

He used the Twelfth Street door because he didn't want to go past the stolen car that was parked on Pearl Street. They walked side by side with Alex's gun pointing towards Rosita's pelvic region.

Herman had just parked his cab at the intersection of Twelfth and Mount Vernon Streets, one block north of Pearl. He removed the ignition key from the dash before entering the cigar store to make a call. There was music coming from a radio in the store — 'I wish you shelter from the storm, a cozy fire to keep you warm and most of all, when snowflakes fall I wish you love.'

"How are you, Mildred?" he asked as she answered the phone.

"All right. I'm waiting for Harry to come home." Mildred laughed.

Oh no, Herman thought. *It's worse than I thought.* "It's Herman, Mildred. I'll be home in about three hours for a bite."

"Everything will be ready," she said, still laughing.

"See you then." Herman hung up, thoughtful about what he should do about Mildred.

As he came out of the store, he saw the couple walking towards the cab. It was strange that the man walked slightly to the rear of the girl. The message was ominous.

They reached the cab all at the same time. Alex pulled his gun and peered into the front of the cab.

A light snow was falling as the man asked, "Where's the key?" He pointed the gun at Herman.

Rosita looked at Herman with such a hopeless expression that Herman realized she was a hostage. He reached inside the cab.

"Hey, what are you up to?" growled the gunman.

"The key," Herman answered, pointing towards the glove compartment, but instead going quickly to the floor and picking up a jack handle. He turned and with all his strength be brought the handle down on the ankle of the abductor.

A devilish sound like a howl came from the beast of a man. In the darkness he fired directly at Herman with the .38 caliber gun.

Herman felt himself going. He looked at Rosita, his face as white as the snow, but he managed to spurt out the words, "Tell them to take care of Mildred," before he sunk to the ground. There was a gasp. Poor Herman, who had just begun a new life, shook his thighs together violently, his head shook from side to side and his eyes bulged. There would be no medicine that could stop this last convulsion. The bullet had entered his chest.

Dr. Miguel had freed himself from the bonds, and he opened the door on Twelfth Street. He saw one of his patients with a very excited look.

Sergo Valdez waved to the doctor, and said, "There's a man with a gun holding a girl on the corner at Mount Vernon Street." It was a Spanish speech in a fast cadence.

"Sergo, *llamar polcia,*" said the doctor. He explained to Sergo that his phone was useless.

Dr. Miguel ran back into his office, picked up a bottle of water-colored liquid marked 'Flammable.' He got a large wad of absorbent cotton, then ran up the alley that was adjacent to his building and led into Mt. Vernon Street.

The traffic was extraordinarily light on this evening and Alex was furious. He was waiting for a car to stop at the stop sign. He griped to Rosita, "Goddamnit, where's all the cars?"

Alex was busy looking the other way when Dr. Miguel sneaked onto the corner from the alley. He raised his knee to the small of the gunman's back, preseed it in with force and applied the wad which was soaked with ether to the nose of Alex. As the kidnapper got weak, the doctor retained a firm grip on his throat. Alex slumped to the ground, letting his gun fall. A police cruiser appeared at the scene at that instant.

Rosita filled in the officer with what she knew, ending with, "He was very brave."

"Poor Herman," the doctor commented.

"You knew him? Rosita questioned.

"Yes. He was my patient."

Rosita hestiated before saying, "Doctor, then perhaps you know a Mildred. His last words were 'Tell them to take care of Mildred.' "

"I don't know of a Mildred, but I'll ask his friend, Adolph. Maybe he can shed some light on the matter."

The police ordered a van to take Herman's body to the morgue, and handcuffed Alex. Rosita and the doctor were asked to go along to the precinct station.

Dr. Miguel requested to take the ether back into the office, and also, he had a few patients to look after.

Rosita spoke up, "It was very valorous to help the way you did." She offered her hand to the doctor.

"I enjoyed doing it for you, Rosita. Perhaps I shall see you at the station."

Rosita was not detained at the station very long. She answered he questions for the investigation, and was booked as a material witness in the murder of Herman. She would be the plaintiff in the kidnapping. Her father came to pick her up, and said he was not going to let her out of his sight for a long while.

Dr. Miguel came to the station later, but was not detained long.

A policeman rang the bell at Herman's house. When Mildred answered, the officer was very gentle. "I have bad news to report about Herman Soler."

Mildred watched very carefully at the cop's lips moved. She said, "Bad news? It wasn't Harry?"

"Oh no." the cop answered. The cop realized that Mildred was just a woman whom Herman had picked up. "Is there anyone else in the house?"

"No, just me." Mildred giggled.

"Can I come in for a minute?" the cop asked.

"All right. I guess so."

The officer had had experience in such cases as this, so he went immediately to a table where the telephone stood. He found a note on the table, showing the address of Herman's sister, with a notation that she would be notified in case of an emergency.

"This will help," he said aloud. "A relative usually identifies the body. I can call his sister, can't I?" he asked.

Mildred stood watching the officer's lips, and still puzzled, said, "Phone, yeah. I guess so."

The sister advised the cop she would take the hour's ride the next day to take care of things.

The following day, Ms. Houseman, Herman's sister, went to the morgue and identified her brother's body, then went to the house at Tenth and Pearl which now belonged to her.

Ms. Houseman questioned Mildred. "How long have you known

Herman?'' she asked.

"Not long," Mildred answerd in a weak tone.

"What's your name?"

"Mildred Springer."

"Where were you living before?"

Mildred thought for a while before saying, "Out in the country, but I'd like to go back to Kensington."

Ms. Houseman thought that Mildred responded rather unusually, but then again her brother used to give her some strange answers too.

She saw a list of telephone numbers on the end table, and decided to call the first one, which was Adolph's.

Adolph answered the phone.

"Do you know a Mildred Springer?" Ms. Houseman asked.

"No, the name doesn't sound familiar," said Adolph.

"Did you know Herman very well?"

"I think I can say that I did," Adolph answered.

"I'm Ms. Houseman, Herman's sister, and I would like you to come over for a while."

"I'd be glad to. I'll be right over."

When Adolph arrived at the corner house, Ms. Houseman introduced him to Mildred.

Adolph also thought that Mildred acted in a strange manner, and he felt sorry for her.

"You can call me Adolph," he said to Ms. Houseman.

"I hate to bother you, Adolph, but I must explain. I'll be so busy this week making arrangements for the funeral, trying to do something about this house and so forth," she looked at Mildred. "I don't think I can let Mildred stay here very long. I want to sell this place."

"I have a vacant room now," Adolph turned to Mildred but did not get a response, so asked, "Would you like a room in my house, Mildred?"

"I guess I can stay anywhere until I get to Kensington," she replied. Then when she saw that Adolph was puzzled, she said, "Yes."

Ms. Houseman nodded her head in relief. She felt she would be responsible if anything happened to Mildred in a three-story house by herself.

"Did Herman give you a key to the house?" she asked.

"I don't have any keys," Mildred answered, laughing.

Ms. Houseman found a suitcase in the front room, and packed her few clothes. She had only the clothes Herman had bought for her.

"I thank you very much, Adolph," said Ms. Houseman.

"I'm glad to help out," Adolph replied just as the phone rang.

It was Dr. Miguel, and he inquired, "Does anyone know a Mildred?"

"I'm Herman's sister. Mildred is here, but she's getting a room at Adolph's up the street. Would you like to speak with him?"

"Yes."

Ms. Houseman handed Adolph the phone.

"Adolph, this is Dr. Miguel. Rosita told me that the last wish of Herman's was that Mildred should be given good care."

"Don't worry, Doctor. I'm taking her to my house, and she can stay as long as she wants."

"Thank you."

Adolph hung up and turned to Ms. Houseman. "That was Dr. Miguel, a friend of Herman's, and that Herman wished Mildred would have good care. I'll see to that, Ms. Houseman."

"Thanks. You're a wonderful man, Adolph."

Adolph led Mildred out of the door and towards his house.

After Mildred was seated in the living room, she asked, "Do you get the paper?"

Adolph didn't have one, so he went to the corner and bought a newspaper. He came home and handed it to Mildred, who immediately looked at it and said, "It's Thursday. I thought it was Wednesday." She still recalled that Herman had told her earlier in the day that it was Wednesday.

The phone rang, and Adolph answered it. It was Rosie, Herman's old girl friend. She said, "I heard that Herman got killed. Would you please come up to my apartment. I have something that belonged to him."

"How do I get up there?" asked Adolph.

"It's easy. Just take the bus on Girard Avenue, then take the El. I live a half block from the El."

Adolph hung up, but quickly used the phone again to call his niece.

"Will you come over tonight, Jeanne? I have an errand to do."

Jeanne was at Adolph's promptly at seven, and Adolph introduced them by saying, "Mildred, here's my niece, Jeanne. If you want anything just tell her. I'll be back in a couple of hours."

It was seven fifteen when Adolph entered Rosie's apartment in the Frankford section. Rosie brought a bottle of V.O. to the table.

"That bum is better off dead," she said.

"I wouldn't talk that way about Herman, Rosie. He was trying hard to make it. He even got a job on the cabs, and was working steady. He died saving the life of the Torresse girl."

Rosie stared at Adolph as though she didn't believe him. "Take a drink, Adolph," she said.

"I can't stay long, Rosie. I have a new tenant I want to check on."

They talked about Herman for a while, and had another drink.

"Are you going to the funeral, Rosie?"

"No way. When I think of the money I spent trying to make him a man, I get sick. I'm not going," Rosie assured him. After Rosie took the third drink, she started to feel good. She scooted closer to Adolph and felt him, finally taking it out. "It's a round one just like Herman's," she said. "Let's go on the sofa."

Adolph got impatient. "It's no use. It won't get hard. I'd better get going."

"Hold it. I'll show you something." Rosie went to the closet and brought out a gadget. "Herman couldn't get his hard most of the time either, so he used this cock extender. I paid for the damn thing though. It's a nine incher and cost seventy-five dollars."

She explained to Adolph how to put it on. "You have to put some of this on." She got a jar of Vaseline and applied it to the plastic hollow tube that went over Adolph's dick.

He had the belt-like strap around his waist and was ready for the action. He wasn't so keen about it first, for he didn't know what he would get out of it, but when she started to heave her belly and make sounds, Adolph got a boot from it.

"Oh . . . that's good," Rosie said at the climax.

"I've got to get back," Adolph said.

"I would like you to take the cock extender with you. I didn't want it in the first place."

"What am I going to do with it?" questioned Adolph.

"You can use it on any woman. You can even use it on me again if you want too. You see, Adolph, if I croak, I wouldn't want them to find it in my apartment. It's not so bad if it's found in a man's house."

Adolph thought for a while. He had wanted one of those gadgets for a long time, but didn't have the seventy-five dollars to spend on one. "All right. Put it in a bag, and I'll take it," he said.

"Let's have something to drink first," Rosie suggested.

"Just one more," Adolph agreed.

It was ten o'clock when Adolph got home.

Mildred had already retired for the night, and Jeanne didn't know how to say it. "She tries so hard to be nice. but she forgets so many things," Jeanne said.

"Well, we'll see how she gets along tomorrow," Adolph said. "Thanks a lot for your trouble."

"Good night, Uncle," Jeanne placed a kiss on his cheek.

Mildred seemed to do all right the next day, but maybe it was because she spent a lot of time just petting the dog. The particular thing she enjoyed doing was washing the dishes. Then, of course, she would want to see the newspaper. She looked at the top of the pages mostly so she could hold the day in her mind — Friday. Mildred went with Adolph and Dr. Miguel to the services on Saturday. They stopped and picked up Jeanne first.

Rosita Torresse, Ms. Houseman and her husband and some of Herman's taproom friends were there also.

The priest, a tall man with a VanDyke beard lived next door to Herman. He had noticed the change in Herman — noticing his walk was much steadier and his health improved. "Ladies and Gentlemen," he eulogized. "Herman Soler is going to his final reward in Heaven. Anyone who knew him would say he tried very hard in his last days on earth to do the right thing. About his courage, there is no question. He could have given in to the gunman's wishes, been less involved for sure, but he was moved to thwart the kidnapper's attempt to use the young girl to obtain money." The priest took a drink of water. "I might add he did it with the full knowledge that for the first time in many years he was gaining in health. The community should remember him as a true martyr." The priest bowed his head with an "Amen."

Herman's sister sobbed. Mildred looked puzzled as the rest of the group sat with bowed heads.

There was a brief ceremony at the gravesite in Mount Vernon Cemetery, three miles from Adolph's house. Herman was laid to rest beside his mother and father.

Dr. Miguel treated everyone afterwards to dinner at a nearby restaurant. He watched Mildred although not very intently, and noted that although she had a distraught appearance on the surface, she would be attentive if someone was really close to her.

She would try hard to agree or disagree with that person as though she were trying to find out which way the wind was blowing. This she would do by watching, and sometimes repeating what her questioner would say.

The doctor realized that Herman might have been worried about Mildred's condition when he made his last wish, but knew it was not the right time or place for his professional service.

Adolph insisted on paying the check, but Dr. Miguel took it. Looking toward Mildred, the doctor said, "Hold on to your money, Adolph. You may need it." He was sorry he had said that so he quickly added, "Some other time, Adolph. I can't explain now."

CHAPTER 17

Adolph and Mildred walked to the corner and entered the Lutheran Church. It was time for Sunday Mass. Adolph's niece was already there, and was glad to see them.

After the sermon, Adolph and Mildred stopped in with Jeanne at her house and had a friendly visit and ate breakfast.

Afterwards, they watched cartoon shows, and at eleven that morning Adolph wished his niece a good day. He and Mildred left, going to the corner newsstand and bought a paper.

Mildred was happy looking at all those pages with Sunday's date on, and she acted as usual the rest of the afternoon. She got up to make some coffee. Although she could read the labels on everything, she'd get mixed up. She didn't know what she did the minute before, but waited for clues from someone.

That's percolated coffee," said Adolph when she poured the hot water over it. "Use the instant." He reached over and handed it to her.

Mildred laughed. "Yes, instant," she said.

After supper, Mildred kept busy with the dishes, and strangely enough she did a nice, neat job.

Later on, they sat watching TV. Adolph glanced at Mildred and thought she had a young body, younger than his niece. He kept thinking, *not bad, not bad at all*. His attention was no longer on the TV program. His mind was again sex oriented, and he recalled his prolonged efforts with his niece years ago. He moved closer to Mildred.

"Do you mind if I shut the set off?" he asked. "I'd like to talk to you."

"What?" Mildred asked. She had not watched Adolph's lips.

"Can I talk to you?" he repeated.

"Yes, you can talk," she said.

Adolph shut the set off and asked, "What was Herman like?"

"Herman?" Mildred didn't understand.

"Yeah, you know, the man who had the corner house, the man who got killed last Wednesday."

"Oh, the corner house. Yes. He didn't play hide the weenie so good!"

"Hide the weenie!" Adolph said.

"Yes. Harry was good when he lived in Kensington."

Adolph moved closer to her. He lifted her dress, and found her skin was nice and smooth. Much smoother than Rosie's. *Boy, he liked it!*

On the way to the bedroom he thought of how Ronnie did it to Angel, and to him. Then that sex literature from New York and California with the pictures of all those dicks came to mind. They had a gadget that was placed over the cock and then air was pumped in. The pictures would then show how the penis would change in size, but the pictures were always of young guys. *What about the old guys?*

Adolph got hot in a hurry — at least in the head, and he took off his clothes. He then asked Mildred to take off hers.

"Yours is not like Harry's," she said. "You got a round one. Harry had a point on his, but yours is like the man on the corner."

"You mean Herman?"

Mildred had to think again. "Herman — he had a little one like you. He made me cry. He wanted to put his weenie in my mouth. Harry . . . Harry, in Kensington, he had a big one, but he never did that."

"I would never do that either," Adolph consoled. He was thinking about Harry, the guy with the big one. He went to the drawer of the dresser where he had placed the cock extension. It had to be as big as Harry's for it was a nine incher!

All the lights were out, and Adolph greased up the gadget. He hooked it up to his waist and was ready.

Mildred knew how to wrap her medium long legs around him, and Adolph started pumping. Her stomach heaved and she groaned blissfully. As her vagina filled with fluid, she sighed. "It's been a long time," then suddenly went haywire. She grabbed Adolph by the neck, and shouted, Harry, Harry from Kensington." Harry on the Main Line had not given her much loving.

Adolph had to struggle to free himself from her grasp. "That's it for the night," he said. He was already going sour about the whole thing. After all, what was he getting out of it?

They were in the kitchen later, and Adolph gave Mildred a glass of milk. "You need some nourishment," he said, smiling.

After watching the late movie, they went to bed.

Ms. Houseman had just finished breakfast in her stone front house in Hatboro and was looking through the paper when her eye caught the following?

> On Wednesday, Harry Springer was on his way to talk to a doctor in Kensington about his mentally ill wife, Mildred. At Eighth and Allegheny, a dangerous intersection, his car collided with a truck and he was killed instantly. On the same day, his wife went out of the house and has not returned. A son, Ralph has supplied police with pertinent information, but as yet there have been no photos available, and her whereabouts is unknown. They live in Bala-cynwyd. They formerly resided in Kensington.

"Oh my God," Ms. Houseman cried out. "That's the name of that woman who stayed in my brother's house." She immediately got on the phone and called Adolph.

"Oh, I'm so excited, Adolph. I read in the paper that that woman, Mildred, is most likely a poor lost soul. I thought she was flaky. Her name is Springer, and she's been missing since Wednesday. Ask her if she knows Harry. He was killed in an accident."

"Yeah. She's been talking about a Harry a lot. Harry from Kensington," said Adolph.

"You'd better call the police. Her son is looking for her."

"I'll call them right away. Thanks for calling, Ms. Houseman."

Adolph went immediately to the paper, and it made him feel like an old man. The whole story was there. He handed the paper to Mildred and asked, "Is your last name Springer?"

"Springer," she said just like that. And her next word was "Yes."

Adolph called the police and told them Mildred Springer was at his house.

Ralph Springer was in the Bala police station when the report came through that his mother had been located. He and a cop hopped in the police car and went to Adolph's.

When they arrived, Mildred was looking at the newspaper, but had not gotten to the second page yet, where the article was.

Adolph took the paper from her and told her that her boy was waiting for her. She got up and said, "Boy."

"Mom. Am I glad to see you." Ralph rushed to his mother, but saw her distraught. "I'm your son, Ralph."

She watched his lips carefully, "Ralph, yes, Ralph."

Ralph had a picture album under his arm and he showed his mother a picture of his father.

"Look, Mom. Here's pop," she said.

Mildred put her hand on the picture and said, "Harry, yes, Harry from Kensington." She looked at Ralph. "Are you going to take me to Harry in Kensington?"

The tears came. He couldn't hold back any longer.

"Why would you cry?" Mildred recalled the phrase that Adolph had used the night before.

Ralph looked at the cop who lowered his eyes sadly. "It's because I found you. I'm glad that you're all right. It's Valentine's Day, and I'm happy, Mom. We're going home." Ralph took his mother by the arm and the cop took her by the other arm. They walked towards the door.

Another officer asked Adolph questions and Adolph told him how he met Mildred. He told him he could check it out with Ms. Houseman.

Adolph was sad as he realized Mildred was really leaving.

The officer took Adolph's phone number, saying, "Just in case, but I don't think you'll have to go to the station."

CHAPTER 18

It was a week after Valentine's day and Adolph still felt terrible that he had even got mixed up with that futile sex obsession. He didn't practice yoga anymore. He forgot to put on his leotards. He was beginning to look like the old man he was when he pushed the broom around, working in the liquor store.

Adolph looked under the dining room table where his faithful dog, Spot, was sitting. Poor Spot was nearly twelve. He didn't come running to his master, and he was losing his hearing. He also had a cataract in his left eye. There wasn't much Adolph could do to help the dog, but give him Vitamin A pills. Adolph never let the dog go out by itself, fearing it would run away.

The previous Saturday, Adolph had gone to the Torresse Market to catch Rosita, but had missed her, and he was going to try again today.

He put on his coat, patted Spot on the head, saying "I'll give you some chicken when I get back." He took the Bible from the table and put it under his arm. Spot got up and wagged his tail as Adolph started for the door.

Rosita met Adolph when she got out of her car. She saw a depressive looking man with a Bible clutched under his arm.

"Please, Rosita. I have something important to tell you," Adolph spoke up.

She recognized him from the funeral, and said, "Yes?"

"I have a confession to make." He stammered a bit, then continued. "It wasn't Ronnie, you know, Dr. Miguel, in bed with Elba. It was me. I'm the dirty old man responsible for what happened. Dr. Miguel was in the room first, but he left the room in the dark, and that's when I took his place. Elba didn't know the difference because she drank some hundred proof liquor. Please, Rosita, give the doctor a break." Adolph bowed his head.

"I saw you at the funeral," Rosita said. "What is your name?"

"Just call me Adolph."

"Well, Adolph. I thank you for what you have told me. It was very nice of you."

"When will you speak to him?" Adolph asked.

"I'm not really sure. I want a little time to think."

"I hope it's soon. God bless you, Rosita."

Rosita waved good-bye as she walked toward the market.

As soon as he got home, Adolph called Dr. Miguel.

After listening, the doctor exclaimed, "Well, I'll be. Whatever made you do that, Adolph?"

"I owe it to you, Doctor. It was my duty. I think you have a good chance of getting her back now," Adolph said.

"You're so super, Adolph, and I'm grateful to you. I won't forget it."

After Adolph's call, Dr. Miguel used the phone immediately.

"Rosita," he asked, "will you be kind and let me talk to you?"

"I was going to call you," said Rosita. "Yes, I think we should talk it over."

"I have no appointments on Wednesday night. Will that be all right?"

"All right. I'll pick you up with my beetle. I love to drive," answered Rosita.

"Would you care to stop at Patano's?" the doctor asked.

"It's all right with me," Rosita agreed.

Rosita pulled up to the doctor's home on Wednesday evening. The doctor came down the steps, got into the car and sat beside the exotic-looking girl. She wore a red dress and black pantyhose.

Dr. Miguel wore a checkered coat and slacks to match. They talked about their dates when they first met while they drove to Patano's. The parking lot attendant handed Rosita the ticket.

Dr. Miguel pushed the revolving door, and they entered the cafe to the tune, *I Wish You Bluebirds in the Spring, But More Than This I Wish You Love.*

"We'll take a sip of wine first," Ronaldo suggested. "Would you prefer a May wine or a Rhineskeller Rhine?"

"May wine?" Rosita questioned. "I've never heard of it."

"It's a very light wine, unique in aroma and taste. It's classed as miscellaneous," explained the doctor.

"Either will be okay with me as long as it's not something like that Southern Comfort. My dad doesn't want me to drink that hundred proof stuff," Rosita explained.

"Your dad knows," the doctor laughed, "but actually it's not all that bad. You just don't drink too much of it. It's really bourbon and peach brandy combination."

The doctor decided on the chicken dinner, and Rosita ordered the same.

Patano's was out of the May wine.

"It's too bad. I wanted you to taste it. I guess we'll take the Rhine. That'll do good with the chicken."

"That's all right, Ronnie. Whoops, or shall I call you Doctor?"

"Ronnie's ideal. Remember we're old friends." The doctor patted her hand.

Rosita tasted the Rhineskeller Rhine. "It's not sweet; just right," she said.

The aroma of oregano and basil hit the nostrils, but the olive oil and butter kept the tasty dish close to a bland type. A fresh salad made the dinner even more enjoyable.

After the meal, they attended a movie at a nearby drive-in.

Ronaldo was getting that warm feeling that was present in his dates with Rosita long ago. The musical show was a two-hour film and very heart warming.

As they rode out of the parking lot, Ronnie said, "I'd like to see you often, Rosita."

"Let's talk about it later. I'd like you to meet my parents first."

She drove down the boulevard, over Rising Sun to Sixth, then on to Fourth, where the car came to a halt in front of a colonial type structure in the Society Hill section.

"We live only about a mile from your office," she informed him.

Rosita unlocked the door and they entered the living room where Michael Torresse and his wife were watching TV.

After the introductions, Torresse showed his disappointment in the way his son behaved, by saying, "I wanted Angel to be a doctor, but why should I bother anyone . . .?"

Angel was working on a relatively unimportant job in the super market and had secured an apartment for himself.

Mr. Torresse was round-faced, had a mustache and wore eyeglasses with thick, black plastic frames. He said, "Why don't we have some Harvey's Bristol Cream?"

The maid brought the sherry into the room on a cart that had everything on it that was necessary to serve the wine. They chatted and drank, and were not very absorbed in what was on the TV screen.

"I don't want you to drive this late, Rosita, so I'll have only one glass of the wine now," said Torresse.

"I can go with you," said the girl.

"Sure, Toots," answered her father.

After the conversation and refreshment, Mr. Torresse led his daughter and the doctor to the car. They all got into his Cadillac — Rosita and the doctor sat in the back.

As they neared the doctor's house, Ronnie gave Rosita a kiss and said, "The next meal we have we'll drink Creme Yvette. It's made with violets, and reminds me of you."

"You flatter me," said Rosita.

"Good night, and thanks a lot, Mr. Torresse."

Dr. Miguel and Rosita dated all that Spring, and at the start of Summer, they were engaged. The doctor suggested they have the wedding before the trial of the kidnapper so they would have time for the honeymoon.

The wedding took place in October. Mr. Torresse hired chauffeured El Dorados for the occasion. One of the cars was used to pick up the doctor, another went for Adolph and Jeanne.

Michael accompanied his daughter, in white velvet gown, to the altar, and the priest of the Bonaventure Church gave the marriage vows. Now man and wife, the groom took Rosita down the aisle and out the door.

A large wedding dinner was prepared. The guests ate salads, relishes along with tiny loaves of pumpernickel. For the enjoyment of the group, there was a meal which consisted of broiled lamb chops with fresh buttered broccoli and creamy little lumps of potatoes. A combination of whipped cream and nutty cake went well with the coffee for dessert.

Adolph did not feel like dancing when the music began to play, but wished that Jeanne would. "Look, Jeanne. There's a man sitting by himself. Why don't you ask him for a dance?"

"I just don't have nerve," answered Jeanne.

"Well, I will," said Adolph going to the other table.

The man was pleased to dance with Jeanne as the *Alley Cat* was playing.

They danced, and when the music stopped, they sat with Adolph who had watched their dance steps and he told them they were great.

"My son said Mr. Torresse wanted a big crowd so he brought me along with him," said Jeanne's dancing partner.

"Did your son go to the same school as Dr. Miguel?" asked Adolph.

"My son is an intern at the University of Pennsylvania Veterinary School," said Dr. Milton Stern, handing his card to Adolph. "He wants to be in the same profession as his father."

"I've got a sick dog, but no car to take him to your place on Broad Street," said Adolph.

"Do you live near Jeanne? I was going to take her home, but she said she has transportation."

"Yes. I live at 903 Pearl Street. I'm Adolph Teitleman — you can call me Adolph."

"Well, Adolph, I don't usually go into that neighborhood, but I could for a friend of Dr. Miguel."

"Fine, Dr. Stern. I'll be calling you," Adolph said.

"And, I'll be calling you," said the vet, turning to Jeanne.

Jeanne was too surprised to say anything. She pulled in her chin just a trifle, and said, "All right, Doctor."

"You can call me Milton," Dr. Sterns said.

The bride and groom came to their table and wished them good-bye as they left for their honeymoon in Hawaii.

CHAPTER 19

It was the news hour, but Adolph made no attempt to turn on the TV set. Adolph was resting and thinking. He was glad that his niece had met a nice man, and he sincerely hoped and prayed that things would work out well for her.

The pains in his chest was bad news, for that's the way his wife and his father went.

"What would become of Jeanne when he died?" he said to himself. When he hit on the lottery, he gave some thought of moving, then he asked Jeanne to get a place in another neighborhood, but they still stuck close by to the Lutheran Church. Adolph changed his will to read that Jeanne would only get his money if she moved to a better neighborhood when he died.

Adolph got up from his rocker and went to the bureau drawer, took out the artificial nine-inch cock and put it in his coat pocket. He went out into the street and up to the corner. There was nobody on the street. He threw the dick extender down the sewer, thankful that no one saw him, and walked back home.

He sat again in his rocker and thought. *"Where was all the sweet-smelling romance? Were the old guys supposed to get any, or were they just supposed to be dirty old men?"* He glanced at the picture of himself and his wife when they were just married — that was sweet.

In thoughts he was propelled to his working days at the liquor store — the wise guys; the endless sex jargon; an atmosphere that suggested easy sex, and why not get some of it? Finally he thought of a guy who wanted to soothe things, so he said, "Keep a cool head and a warm bosom."

Three weeks went by and Dr. Stern dated Jeanne three more times. He was talking to her on the third date. "I lost my wife five years ago, and I'm thinking of getting remarried."

Jeanne felt she should tell the doctor herself rather than allow him to hear it from somebody else. She told him all about the time she got raped.

"Poor girl," he said. "I'm the one who can rightly sympathize with you Jeanne." He turned for a brief moment and said, "You see, my wife was also raped, and the beast murdered her."

"Oh my God! They're animals with no bit of humanity. They're worse than animals, walking the street," Jeanne tearfully recounted.

"Aren't you scared when you go out?" asked the vet.

Jeanne put back her handkerchief and said, "All the time. I keep looking back even when I go to the store."

"Jeanne. You're too nice to stay in this neighborhood all your life. I'd like to see you move to a better place."

"Is that a proposal?" she asked.

"Yes, if you are willing."

"We have a date for next week, so let's talk about it then, Milton."

"Fair enough, and do have a good week, Jeanne."

"Until next week then, bye," Jeanne waved as he left.

Adolph called Dr. Stern in the early evening on Wednesday. The doctor examined Spot and told Adolph there wasn't much that could be done for the dog. He was too old. There was no cure for the cataract nor for his deafness.

When Adolph told the doctor the dog had taken a fit when he was a pup, but pulled through after six visits to a doctor, Dr. Stern suspected cancer but said nothing to Adolph. The doctor gave Adolph some ointment that could be squeezed into the dog's eyes to counteract the mucous, and also some pills to be administered. He charged Adolph only ten dollars for his visit.

"That's my fee at the office, but you're a friend, and I won't ask any more," explained the doctor.

"Thanks's but here's twenty. You are very kind," said Adolph.

"No, I won't accept anything over ten." The doctor put a ten back in Adolph's pocket.

"Listen, Doc. I can afford it. I just hit on a number not long ago in the lottery. At the risk of sounding silly, I'd like to offer you a nice sum as a wedding gift if you marry my niece."

'The doctor smiled, then laughed loudly.

"What's so funny? I want to see her in safe hands before I die. She had something terrible happen to her, and I don't care to have her live through something like that again."

"She told me all about it, Adolph. The funny part is that I'm about to propose to her. I don't need to be bought into it."

"Oh, God bless you and keep you. I wish you luck all your life."

"Thank's, Adolph. Call me if I can be of any help."

"Yes. I can never forget you. Good night, Doc."

It was a nice day in November of 74 when Jeanne visited her uncle. He had just finishing cooking some chicken and was cooling a piece off by running cold water on it. Spot didn't grab it as he usually did, but circled around it several times before he chewed on it. He seemed to even have trouble chewing.

"He has a lot of trouble trying to chew," Adolph said.

"What did the doctor say about that?" Jeanne asked.

"He left some pills that I give him, but Spot doesn't chew any better."

"You know Milton wants to get me an apartment in Elkins Park so I can stay there until we get married next year."

"Well, Jeanne. What did you tell him?"

"I told him I'd stay. We're getting married in our church, Adolph. A tragedy can happen anywhere I guess. Milton lives in the northeast which is acclaimed as a good place, but his wife was murdered by a rapist there."

"When do you expect to get married?" Adolph stooped in his chair to feed Spot some biscuits when he gave a cry. He was out of breath and pointing to his breast.

"I'll call the doctor," Jeanne said. She then helped Adolph to the sofa and fixed the cushion for him.

Dr. Miguel arrived in fifteen minutes. When he examined Adolph's blood pressure, the sphygmomanometer read 150 over 90 which was on the border line. He gave Adolph a needle for fast relief, then wrote a prescription for nitroglycerin tablets.

"I don't want you to do anything requiring exertion. Don't go up the steps," the doctor turned to Jeanne and she nodded. "When you feel that pain, take the medicine," he advised. He shook hands with Adolph before leaving.

"I guess I can answer your question about the wedding, Adolph. We want to have it in April."

Adolph was feeling better already, and said, "There's something I want to do about my will, Jeanne. First, when I can go out, I have to strike out the provision that you must move in order to become my beneficiary, then I would like to leave a gift just in case I'm not around to make it to the wedding."

"Oh, Uncle Adolph. You'll be all right, don't worry."

"You never know what can happen in six months," Adolph warned.

"I'm glad I decided not to move. I can help you with the house-work until you get stronger."

"That's very nice, Jeanne. I'm so glad you're getting a good hus-band."

"I've got to be going, so call me if you need me, Adolph."

Two days later Dr. Miguel found Adolph's condition improved and cut the heart medicine dosage in half. He prescribed a diuretic and told Adolph to see him in a week.

On Monday Adolph took care of the change in his will, but decided against leaving a wedding gift in the will. He decided to put himself back in shape. He started to wear. the leotards, and he took more vitamins and tried Yoga again.

On Friday he saw the doctor. He was told he only had to come to the office once a month thereafter.

On his December visit, Adolph did so well that the doctor told him to discontinue the heart medicine and use it only if he had the pain. The diuretic would be on a maintenance level.

Before Christmas, Adolph received a beautiful card from Ralph Springer. He said his mother, Mildred, was recovering from her ner-vous condition. She had required sedation when told of her hus-band's death, but was getting along all right now. He thanked Adolph for caring for his mother.

Ralph's card made Adolph's heart a little lighter because Herman's last wish had been fulfilled. Adolph prayed Mildred would say no-thing about the weenie extension.

Adolph was so anxious to see Jeanne married that he took no chances in going down to Broad Street on this cold New Years Day to see the Mummers Parade. He watched it on TV so he could be warm.

It was a March day, and Adolph had just received his mail. Most of the junk mail he got was of a sexual nature. This day they were out gunning for him again. There was an ad and literature on another gadget to transform an old penis into a new one or rather a young one. This time it was a pendulum type device that was attached to the penis. A young guy with cock lag could use it also. The theory was that the weight would exercise the organ much like dumbbells exercised various parts of the body. The guy would end up with more muscle in his penis for an erection.

Adolph read all the material even though he would not buy anything. There were pictures of guys with their tools hanging before using the gadget and after. Adolph wondered why they never showed old guys in the pictures, but he was sure they had a reason. He had no intention of experimenting with any cock-hardeners after his heart trouble. His niece was getting married in three weeks, and he thought he should forget the sex stuff for the present.

He gathered all the printed matter of the sexually oriented ad and threw it into the rubbish basket. He thought of having a bit of fun by going fishing, so he called his old friend, Al Notiso.

"It's about that time, Al," he said. "How about throwing out a line?"

"The time is right, Adolph, but I'm not. I've got that lousy arthritis, and it's bothering me too much."

"Oh, I'm sorry to hear that, Al. I know about pains. I had those heart pains not long ago. Hope you get better soon."

"Thanks for calling. Maybe we can make it some other time."

"All right, Al. I'll call you later. Bye."

Adolph thought he'd like to play some chess to fill in the time, so he called his niece to tell her he was going to take a walk down to the library. He walked down Pearl Street to Sixth and then slowly took the steps to the entrance of the library.

Inside, he met Phil Dolan who was one guy he could very seldom do anything with. Phil, an elderly man with a bald head, was an expert when it came to chess. The young ones in the neighborhood wouldn't even go to the table to play. He was too tough for them.

Adolph lost two games. He had enough for the day so he went back home.

Adolph took a chicken leg out and offered it to Spot, but the dog circled about, acting as though he didn't want to eat. Adolph had to do a lot of coaxing before Spot took the knuckle off the bone and chewed it. After Spot ate all he wanted, Adolph prepared for the big meal of the day.

During the next three weeks, Adolph had plenty of time to try and beat Phil Dolan in the game of chess at the library, but actually he beat him only one time. And that game Adolph thought Phil gave him because there was a chance of Phil getting a draw. The day Adolph won was just three days before his niece would be married.

The following day when Adolph took a walk up the street, he saw a "For Sale" sign on Jeanne's house. His heart fluttered a while, but then he realized that Jeanne was going to live with Dr. Stern in the Northeast after they were married. He boarded a bus at the corner, got off at Sixth and Market, then walked to a small street above Market that advertised cheap suits.

A salesman tried to sell him an old suit.

"What do you want?" he asked. "A good old suit, or a new suit that's no good?"

Adolph left the store in a hurry. He didn't know why he went in there in the first place. He was determined to get a new suit for Jeanne's wedding. His next stop was Strawbridge's where he got what he wanted. All the suit needed was cuffs and he had them made while he waited.

The marriage ritual was performed on Saturday by the Reverend Brown at the Holy Father's Lutheran Church.

Ralph Springer was the best man, and Uncle Adolph gave the bride away. She wore a lovely ecru-colored gown of satin and lace.

After the ceremony, Adolph noticed how straight Jeanne walked, how solid she looked, and he was proud of her.

The wedding party headed uptown to Chelten Avenue where the reception would be held at Chelten Caterers. Dr. Miguel, and his wife, Rosita, were enjoying themselves as the refreshments were about to be served. Adolph sat at the table with Ralph Springer. He was glad that Ralph didn't bring his mother along.

"How's your mother getting along?" he asked.

"She's getting along fine, but still under medical attention. The doctors said she'd be all right in a couple of months."

"I'm so glad to hear that," Adolph replied.

"The doctor said the fact that we moved back to Kensington had a great benefit on her condition. Her health improved when we settled down in the old neighborhood."

The dinner was somewhat of an anomaly. It consisted of a German-style dish, partridge with champagne, sauerkraut, mushrooms, artichokes, white asparagus, carrots and German noodles. The champagne was Renault Chateau, served just before the dessert which was a serving of strawberries soaked with Grand Marnier.

There was an exchange of partners as they danced, and Ralph Springer, Dr. Miguel, and Dr. Stern had a lot of fun dancing with Rosita and Jeanne.

It was a Thursday, and the trial of Alex Cortez was held. The jury had been picked the day before. Dr. Miguel and his wife were seated in the courtroom in the Federal Building. They didn't have long to wait for the jury to reach a verdict. It took only nine minutes for them to convict Alex.

Alex received a life sentence in the Federal Penitentiary.

It was the beginning of May, and it was the third day that Spot couldn't hold any food. He even threw up chicken. He then stopped trying to eat, and would just drink water, but couldn't hold that either. Adolph tried baby food which also proved futile.

When Spot crawled behind the sofa, Adolph looked at the sheet covering the sofa. The end that had been tucked under the cushion was pulled away.

"Blood," Adolph gasped. *Yeah, it must be from Spot. I didn't see it first,* he thought, *because it was in the corner. Spot was rubbing his nose and working the sheet into the corner of the sofa.*

He looked in the drawer where he had placed Dr. Stern's card. He called the vet, then he found Spot in the corner and brought him out to wait for the doctor. When Adolph sank into his chair, he got that eerie feeling again, a sensation of the blood draining from his body. Inwardly, he called, "Jeanne, Jeanne."

When the doctor arrived, Adolph had Spot close to his side. Dr. Stern saw that Spot was losing his hair and had no interest in life. He made a careful examination. He shook his head. "There's nothing we can do for him now. Spot has cancer."

"Nothing?" Adolph questioned.

"Right, Adolph." The doctor put his hand on Adolph's shoulder. "You'll be doing Spot a favor by calling the ambulance. He can't hear, one eye is gone and the other is clouding up. He's suffering too much, Adolph."

"Thanks for making the call," Adolph said quietly. He gave the doctor two tens, but the doctor quickly shoved one into Adolph's pocket.

The doctor stopped to pet Spot. "You're quite a dog. You'll be going to the 'Fields of Ambrosia!' Good-bye, Adolph."

"So long, Doctor." Adolph saw the doctor to the door.

Adolph was getting that chest pain again when the doorbell rang. It was Rosie, Herman's old girl friend. She was all smiles.

"How've you been?" Adolph asked as he let her in.

"All right, and you?"

"Not so hot, Rosie. What brings you up in this part of town?"

Rosie's unsupported cleavage with the hanging spheres of flesh was an added distraction. She was ugly, and had thin legs. There were not many guys wanting her, so it was no wonder she used to pay bills for Herman in exchange for a little loving.

"I'm gonna call up a guy to give me a thrill, unless you want to, Adolph."

"I'm not up to anything like that now, Rosie. I'm going to call the ambulance for my dog."

"Aw, come on. You got that thing, ain't you?"

"Oh, I threw that away. You said you didn't want it around," Adolph tried to explain.

"I wanted you to keep it for me, you dope. Don't you remember. I said you could use it on me. For that matter, I can get a woman to do it to me with that thing." Rosie picked up the phone directory and threw it on the floor.

Adolph knew Herman was right when he said that Rosie was a schizo.

"You should have stuck that thing up your ass — that's where your brains are," Rosie went on. "I paid seventy-five dollars for it. It was the biggest job they had."

Adolph felt the sharp pain again. He went to his drawer where he kept the money, and counted out seventy-five dollars. "Here's the money, Rosie. I don't want any more trouble. Take it and please go. I don't feel too good."

Rosie looked at the old guy, and seeing he didn't look well, she

114

grabbed the money out of Adolph's hand. "Next time think before you throw stuff like that away. So long."

Adolph was glad to get rid of her, even though it cost. The telephone was ringing, so Adolph walked slowly over to answer it.

"We got back from Canada about an hour ago," said Jeanne. "How are you, Uncle Adolph?"

Adolph paused. He didn't feel like bothering the newlyweds with his problems. "I'm going to call the S.P.C.A. for Spot. The doctor advised me to put him to sleep because he has cancer. There's nothing that can help him now."

Jeanne detected a worried note in Adolph's voice. "Look, Uncle. As soon as we get things together, we'll be down to see you."

"Okay, fine." Adolph put the receiver down slowly.

It was only a half hour after Adolph made the call when the S.P.C.A. truck arrived. It had to be parked on the other side of the street from Adolph's house, for there was no room on the narrow street.

Adolph had Spot in his arms when the doorbell rang. He took a ten dollar bill out of his pocket and handed it to the S.P.C.A. man.

"Let me take him to the truck, please," Adolph said to the man.

The S.P.C.A. man pocketed the ten and said, "Sure, boss. Go ahead."

A crowd of many children and some grown-ups formed as Adolph, his body bent more than ever, walked with Spot. He patted the dog's head, saying, "You're going to the 'Fields of Ambrosia,' " as he placed Spot on the tailgate of the truck.

It was funny that he could remember what he had heard a disgruntled customer say about his marital life. He had said, "Sex is not the 'catch 22' of life!"

Spot stood up straight in the truck, and looked at Adolph with his half-good eye. It was moist.

Adolph used his last bit of strength, and the crowd sensed it. There was not a dry eye in the crowd.

The gate on the back of the truck was not yet closed as Adolph fell to the ground. His last words were, "Good-bye Spot. I wish you love."

Jeanne and her husband drove up and noticed the crowd. They got out of the car, looked at the open door to Adolph's house and then to the people. They could see some leaning over, and Jeanne ran towards the spot where her uncle lay.